Going Down and Moving On

Going Down and Moving On

Charlie Casso

Starr Books

www.UnderTheCherryMoon.com

DEDICATION

This book is dedicated to anyone who has ever held so hard to a dream that it came to fruition or shattered.

CONTENTS

Going Down and Moving On

Chapter One: New Year's Eve: Old Habits Die Hard

Before 2001 becomes the worst of times, it isn't exactly the best of times. Plans to spend New Year's Eve with my Drug-addled Boyfriend mean I must take some precautions, at least prepare myself for the night that will bring me into the new millennium, 2001. To insure myself against an awful New Year's, I ask him, "Are you going to do any drugs while we're out? Because I don't want to ring in the New Year that way, being around you on drugs and all."

He assures me, "Josh, I just want to go out and dance. I promise." I guess I should take him at his word, because who would intentionally want to ruin someone else's New Year's Eve?

Inside Pieces, a small bar in Manhattan's West Village, we check our jackets, exchange hellos with the familiar faces who have come out tonight to celebrate, and make our way to the diminutive area in the bar where people dance around the pool table. An iconic '80s song plays and hands pump in the air to the beat. As I lip sync along with the lyrics, a rift forms between Boyfriend and me.

He asks, "Why would you say that? That's what you think? That you're not my lover, that you're not the one for me? Because I'm such a bad person, because I like to party?"

"Umm, I'm just singing along with the song. Actually, the song is about love. It's a love song. It's a great love song."

"Please, then why does it say you're not my lover? Nice, Josh."

"You're taking the lyrics out of context. It's one of my all-time favorite songs. You should be honored instead of yelling at me because you don't understand the lyrics. The song is about how the person would do anything for his lover, and everything for his lover, without limits."

Boyfriend takes a seat against the wall, crosses his arms against his chest, tilts his head down a bit, clenches his jaw, and stares straight ahead.

"What's wrong?" I inquire.

"Nothing's wrong. Nothing's wrong. I just want to sit down," he replies.

His body language, however, indicates otherwise. Something definitely vexes him, and it's more than the misconstrued song lyrics. I continue to press him, as New Year's Eve shouldn't be a night filled with angst.

He breaks down and admits the issue that affects his mood tonight. "Okay, Josh," he begins, "truth is I want to party tonight. I brought pills with me and I want to take them but I know you'll be mad."

Although he has assured me tonight will be drug-free, he shows me the pocket full of pills he yearns to take. When he exhibits this side of himself, I think of him as my Drug-addled Boyfriend instead of my Boyfriend. I throw my words, "A drug-filled new year is not what I signed up for," and turn toward the coat check. I exchange my coat ticket for my black leather jacket, head toward the door, throw my jacket on as I pass through the door, and walk outside toward Sixth Avenue where the B train can take me back to Brooklyn. Even if I'm on the train when the clock strikes midnight, it will be better to be there alone than here with him.

At the corner of Sixth Avenue, I hear someone run up behind me. Please let it not be a mugger, I pray, as this night has been bad enough already. I brace myself in fear of being attacked, and look over my shoulder to find the person who runs up behind me isn't a mugger. It's worse.

"Josh, Stop."

I reply as I turn to face him, "What? I'd rather be on the train by myself than stay here with you doing drugs."

"Then I'll go with you."

"Why would you go with me? Stay here and do your thing without me. Or don't do your thing and we can both stay here."

"I can't stay here and not take the pills. If I'm here, I want to take the pills."

"So, it's not enough that we're here together? You can't be here just with me? You need me and the pills to be out, is that what you're saying?"

With his fists balled in anger, Drug-addled Boyfriend screeches, "Why does it matter to you? Mister goodie two shoes can't be around people taking drugs? Why do you do this?"

I look directly at his hands, then back to his ice-blue eyes, "Do you want to hit me?" I ask, "Do you really think you're going to touch me? Are you serious?"

He un-balls his fists for a brief moment, then re-balls them and says through clenched teeth, "No, Josh, I'm not going to touch you, you just make me so angry."

A cacophony of screams, cheers, shouts, and horns echoes through the icy night air from every conceivable direction. A clock tower looms above Sixth Avenue and, as I fear I know what I'll see, I look at it anyway. The clock's enormous black hands point at twelve o'clock sharp. Tears gush forth from me with such force they splatter on the ground by my feet, right next to a pink, glitter-adorned, flattened New Year's party hat. My head hangs heavily downward as I watch the tears fall and feel the onset of a headache. Drug-addled Boyfriend exasperates, "Why are you crying?"

Unable to speak, I huddle myself into the doorway of a flower shop, which has its greasy black gates down for the night.

"Josh, why are you crying?" he asks again.

I try to draw in a breath to speak, but to no avail. I try again. "Because, it's New Year's," I whimper as I point my left index finger up toward the clock tower. "It's New Year's. Why tonight? Can't we just have one night without fighting over the same thing? I don't want to do this anymore, I don't think I can take it. This is not how I want to live."

He considers my plea and responds, "But, since we're already out…"

"You've got to be kidding me," I bellow. "Are you serious? Is this a gay man's midlife crisis you're having at twenty-five years old? You're a little old to be partying, but if that's what you want, go for it. Just don't expect me to wait in the wings for you while you try to get your life back together."

Most of the tears dissipate, and I brush off the remaining wetness on my face with the back of my hand. I plant my right foot in front of my left and resume my walk toward the train station at West 4th Street.

I hear, "I want you, Josh. I want you. I don't want anything else. I'll throw the pills out if that's what you want. I want you. Please, let's go home together."

With the power of all of the Greek gods combined with the passion my Italian ancestors are known for, I stop, turn toward his voice, and ask, "Home?"

A smile slowly spreads across my face, not because of his idea to go home, but in spite of it. "You know what?" I ask, "It's New Year's. I want to celebrate 2001. The new millennium's here and I'm not going home. Let's go out. After all, we're already in the city so let's have a good time. Let's go dancing." I start to walk uptown and beckon him forward with my left hand.

"All right! That's more like it," Drug-addled Boyfriend enthusiastically replies as he hurries to catch up. "I don't know why you changed your mind so fast, but I'm glad you did."

We arrive at Splash, a bar in Chelsea known and named for the fact that dancers dance on the bars while water rains down on them from above, and take our place in line to get inside. While in line, Drug-addled Boyfriend questions my change of heart. "Are you sure you want to go to Splash?" he asks as he furrows his blonde-tinted brow. "You never want to come here."

With the utmost conviction, I reply, "Tonight's not just any night, it's New Year's, and I'm going to have a good time tonight."

Five feet into the bar and it's fifty degrees warmer. I immediately peel off my coat and check it at the coat check. "Happy New Year, baby," the coat check attendant wishes me as he presses the coat ticket into the palm of my hand with both of his. He proceeds to kiss me on not one, but both cheeks.

"You know him?" inquires the confusedly contorted face of Drug-addled Boyfriend.

"No," I reply as I shrug it off. Through the corner of my eye I catch the slight curl in his lip as he gives a hard glance at the overly kind, and pretty handsome, coat check attendant.

Three songs' worth of dancing and I already feel my shirt damp with sweat. My arms become wet with the sweat of others who dance shirtless and bump into me on the floor around me. Drug-addled Boyfriend takes his shirt off and fans himself to indicate the oppressive heat generated by the multitude of dancing bodies. I roll my eyes as I look away from him. The heat is not the impetus for him shedding his shirt. His need for attention forces him to discard it, nothing else. Tonight though, this night, the new millennium, needs to start with a new, stronger me, intent on showing him he can't hold me down.

An olive skinned, curly dark-haired stranger locks and loads in on me. His big, brown, bedroom eyes bore into me as he comes nearer. A dangerously sexy smile plays across his face. "Do Italians really do it better?" he asks as he points at my shirt. His left eyebrow moves upward as his stare intensifies.

I feel my cheeks redden and avert my eyes downward. I quickly regain eye contact with him and suggest he decide for himself. He takes my hand in his and, in a raspy voice tinged with a Brazilian accent that ripples through my body, he coos, "Dance with me."

Drug-addled Boyfriend catches wind of this turn of events and materializes at my side. Pointed nose forward, he asks, in the rudest tone imaginable, "Who is this?"

"I don't know, we just met," I reply aloofly.

"What's your name?" I ask the Adonis in wait.

"Fernando." He accompanies the reply with another of his sinisterly sensual smiles. I blush yet again, and this time so does someone else, but with anger.

Drug-addled Boyfriend asks in disgust, "Would you rather dance with this... this… Fernando, Josh?"

"Well, you weren't saying anything, you were just like barely dancing and staring at the lights. He started talking to me and, well, yeah."

"I'm so sorry, Fernando," I offer.

"Don't apologize to him, Josh, you don't owe him anything."

"I don't owe you anything either. You got your shirt off, you're in the club, enjoy. Have yourself a good night. I am."

I move over to Fernando, place my hand on his lower back, and guide him deeper into the middle of the dance floor, flanked by strangers on all sides. Let the music play, let that smile play across Fernando's face, let life play out what it will. Tonight, let me just think about what a new year and a new millennium will bring. And if my inner child high fives me for doing it, knowing things can and will get better, then I can't ask for anything more.

The wealth of possibilities a heartthrob like Fernando inspires, merely by showing interest in me, motivates me to end my relationship with Drug-addled Boyfriend. The break-up lasts for two days. Drug-addled Ex incessantly calls and professes his determination to be done with drugs. He realizes the error of his ways, so he states, and is a changed person.

Chapter Two: A New Year, A New Start

Boyfriend takes both my hands in his and assures me we have an entertaining night out on the town in store for us. "Josh, I know how you feel about the Roxy," he starts, "but I promise tonight it'll just be me and you at the club having a good time. My friend Neal's coming too, and so is his boyfriend. And, just to be honest, they might be doing drugs, but I won't. You're looking at a new me."

A grimace appears on my face upon the mention of drugs. But, rest assured, Boyfriend promises he won't be involved. "Oh," Boyfriend adds, "we may have to make a stop on our way into the city. I think we have to pick up the party supplies."

The grimace makes a reappearance on my face, this time accompanied by an eye-roll at the prospect of having to stop at someone's house to buy "party supplies," A.K.A. drugs, on our way into the city.

I opt to wait in the car while Boyfriend, Neal, and Neal's boyfriend go into what I refer to as the "drug-den," but I'm told by the three faces that appear at my passenger side window, "Oh, no, you have to come in and meet Billie. There's no one else like Billie, you have to see it to believe it." While not a fan of being twelve steps closer to a drug transaction, I concede the matter and approach the door of the two-family house with a sense of impending doom.

Surely, Billie can't hear the doorbell over the music that blares throughout the house, so why even bother ringing the bell at all? The newest Tamia remix rattles the walls. I can't help but wonder what on earth is going on inside. After all, this marks the closest I have come to a drug-den. "This Billie person is never going to hear the bell," I say as I try the handle and find the door unlocked.

Accompanied by the shocked look on Boyfriend's face, I enter the den, projecting, "Hello?"

No response from Billie. Is he dead? This is not how I envisioned my night, ending up on the news at the scene of an overdose. I walk farther in, toward the source of the blaring beat. A leg kicks in the air, a small human form flies four feet off the ground through the open space, and the mane of hair up top whips left to right. I was better prepared to find the victim of an overdose than to find this.

A five-foot vixen of sorts, gender unknown, clad in skin-tight black spandex, flies about the living room to "Stranger in My House," a highly appropriate song given that said vixen seems unaware of anyone else. Arms, legs, hips, and hair are everywhere all at once. Billie doesn't even pause to welcome us, just keeps on dancing as if we aren't there at all. I wonder, did Billie do all of the drugs already?

The four of us stand there, entranced by Billie's movements. They were right, I haven't seen anything like Billie before. As I watch, I realize this scene will forever be etched in my memory as the movements are surely beyond those of any ordinary, non-psychotropic-induced human. As the song nears its conclusion and begins to blend into the next, Billie lowers the volume on the CD player and lands in front of us.

"Hi. You must be Josh."

"I am." (*Although I really want to say: I am mesmerized you are neither Jem nor a Hologram.*)

"I'm Billie. Nice to meet you, Josh."

"Same here. Great dancing. I'm in awe."

"You know I perform, you should come see me. I get you free drink tickets."

Boyfriend offers, "We're all going out tonight, you should come with us. We're going to the Roxy."

"Ay, I can't. I have to do a show tonight, Papi. You boys have fun without me though. I have what you asked for. You wanted ten, you say?"

Boyfriend looks toward Neal and answers, "Ten works, right? Will that be enough, Neal?"

Neal asks, "Umm, well, you said you weren't doing any, is that still the plan?"

At this question, Boyfriend looks right into Neal's eyes like a puppy at its master, asking not to be reprimanded any longer.

"Neal," I begin, "he said he wasn't going to do any tonight."

Boyfriend concedes, "Right. It's probably good to get more than ten, though, so you can hold them for next time."

While he looks at me, Neal voices his decision, "Okay, let's get twenty and I'll hold the leftovers so we don't have to make another trip for a while."

The transaction finalizes as cash exchanges hands for a Ziploc baggie containing pills. When we get in the car, Neal's boyfriend exclaims, "This is so cute, there are little smiley faces on them!" He passes the baggie around the car for everyone to see. I decline, however, as I still want no part of the drugs, especially since I now have the creeping suspicion Boyfriend plans to make use of some of those extra pills. The only question is whether or not he will let me know about it.

I don't have to wait very long for the answer to that question.

As we soar through the Battery Tunnel into the city, Neal suggests everyone partaking in extracurricular activities down their pills now so by the time they arrive at the club they will be reveling in the effects. Neal and his boyfriend down one each, passing a bottle of water between them to help the pills go down. Neal stretches his arm out, the baggie dangling between his fingers in front of Boyfriend. "You in?" he questions.

Boyfriend looks at me and begins, "If I just take one, you won't notice a thing. It just makes me feel happier. I won't act different or anything. You would never even notice if I didn't tell you. I just want to be honest about it."

"You weren't honest before when you said you wouldn't do any tonight, but you want to be honest now? Your timing sucks. I'd rather go home."

"Why do you have to be like that? What are you so scared of? Maybe if you see me take one, and see it doesn't affect me, you won't worry so much about it anymore. You should take one too. We should do it together so you know what it's like."

I wonder, "What, did I morph from an after-school movie in the eighties to present-day?"

I state, "Okay, that's never going to happen."

"All right, sorry. I didn't mean to pressure you to do them, but I do think if you at least saw me take them, you would understand and be fine with it. Just one pill."

"You know what, do what you want. I'd rather you do it than have a bad night because you didn't and then wind up fighting with me about it because I ruined your night. So fine."

With all the glee of a child who finds a puppy under the tree on Christmas morning, Boyfriend exclaims, "You won't regret it, you'll see. This will be great! You'll see how you always worry for nothing, Josh, my little worry-wart."

"Neal, pass me the bottle of water," Boyfriend directs.

Great, I think, on top of everything else now watch him catch herpes from sharing a water bottle with these two.

Twenty minutes later we walk through the doors of the Roxy, pay the entrance fee, have our hands stamped, and proceed onward and inward towards the music. At the bar, Drug-addled Boyfriend pays a few bucks for a bottle of water, even though he could get a well drink for free since it's open bar. He can't mix drinks with his pills, though. A few feet from the bar, Drug-addled Boyfriend repeatedly takes the baggie of pills out of his pocket, puts it back, and takes it out again.

"What are you doing?" I ask.

"Just making sure they're all still there."

Techno music pumps, bodies writhe, and Drug-addled Boyfriend motions toward the mob of shirtless people on the dance floor. "Let's dance," he suggests.

I counter, "How about you dance with your friends for a few minutes? I want to check out the '80s room upstairs first before it gets too crowded."

"Okay, I'll be on the dance floor."

"I'll be right back. Try to keep your shirt on," I reply, hoping that the double-meaning of my words isn't lost on him.

I ascend the stairs to the glass-walled room I refer to as the '80s room that looks out onto the dance floor. Typically, the DJ spins music from the '80s and, once in a while, a song or two from the early '90s. Madonna's "Material Girl" plays when I enter. Alan Cumming dances around with everyone else getting their retro grooves on. From the '80s room, I look out at the dance floor. Drug-addled Boyfriend stands on the sidelines. He does not dance. Instead, he sways back and forth. I wonder, what the hell?

I descend the stairs, pass the bar, and make my way over to him, Neal, and Neal's boyfriend, and discover they all sway, or dance, quite oddly, in a circle. The three of them look as if they just came out of a sweat lodge or something. Their movements are so languid and spatial. In this dance, there seems to be a disconnect between the heads and the bodies in motion. Upon closer inspection, Drug-addled Boyfriend has his eyes closed. He opens them, but his eyelids look incredibly heavy. His eyes close again.

I try to get his attention with a simple, "Hey," but I receive no response.

I try again, "Hey. Helllllo."

Drug-addled Boyfriend replies, with the ever eloquent, "Grunt."

"Are you sleeping? You look like you're going to fall on your face."

"Grunt."

"How many pills did you take? How many pills did you take? Hello?"

"Six? I think."

Drug-addled Boyfriend repeatedly loses his balance, nearly falling forwards or backwards to the floor. Each time I catch him and try to get him to stand straight up, but largely to no avail. He continues to vacillate between two worlds, vertical and horizontal.

"You're going to fall on your face. You can't stand up. Come with me."

I take him by the shoulders and guide him to the bathroom. At the expansive row of sinks, above which are wall-to-wall mirrors, I turn on the cold water.

"Wash your face. Wash your face. Put the water on your face. You're falling asleep."

"Grunt."

"Put the water on your face. Wake up. You need to wake up."

As he attempts to put the water on his face, he complains, "It's cold."

"Good, you need it. Put it on your face. Wake up."

He lays his head on the brim of the sink and claims, "I'm fine."

I clap my hands together sharply and loudly and direct him, "Look in the mirror. Look at yourself in the mirror."

He looks in the mirror, or at least in the direction of the mirror, and once again proffers, "Grunt."

"You look like a mess. Do you see that? This is what drugs do to you."

In my head, I hear, "Now my life is an anti-drug commercial. Great. Where's Alan Cumming? I bet he doesn't have to deal with this."

I spend the next two hours in the Roxy on a couch that likely contains more DNA samples than a decade's worth of Maury Povich shows. Drug-addled Boyfriend sits two feet away from me so I can sporadically get his attention and keep him from falling into sleep or a blackout. Occasionally, a hunky stranger approaches and asks how my night is going, to which I respond truthfully, "I'm babysitting my Drug-addled Boyfriend. And how's your night going?"

While some see this as off-putting and take it as their cue to walk away, others see it as an opportunity to make a move. Which should I choose, a hunky, muscle-bound stranger or my Drug-addled Boyfriend? Additionally, the hunky, muscle-bound strangers can both walk and talk. Score one for them. As much as it would please me to take up one of these offers, I stick with the evil I know and politely decline their advances.

The next morning, not only has Drug-addled Boyfriend's stomach turned, but so have the tables. He demands an answer for my behavior the previous night.

"Excuse me?" I ask.

"You heard me," Drug-addled Boyfriend seethes, "Why were you so mean to me?"

"What? I babysat you on the couch all night. How is that mean?"

"No, Josh. You were cruel. You told me I was a mess and made me look in the mirror."

"I made you look at yourself in the mirror and that's cruel? You *were* a mess. You almost fell on your face, you could barely stand up, and if it weren't for me, you would have blacked out and who knows what else would've happened."

"No, you were cruel. I never thought you'd be like that."

I can't believe he's doing this. This isn't worth arguing about, though. I've got to figure out what to do because I can't take this. As I fight back tears, I manage to get out the words, "I'm sorry."

I feel sorry for the fact I'm still with him, I feel sorry for the fact I don't have the strength to get myself out of this volatile relationship, and I feel sorry for my past and future selves for what I am putting them through. Empathy for him, though, for making him see on this one occasion what I have to see on many, that empathy I don't have. Not sure what exactly to do, I barrel ahead and hope for the best.

A few nights later, in search of a happy place, I suggest we go to The View, a restaurant at the top of the Marriott Marquis in Times Square. The restaurant resides on the impressively high 47th and 48th stories of the hotel. In addition, it has all glass windows and rotates a full three hundred and sixty degrees, affording a complete, breathtaking view of the city. It's an amazing place to go with a loved one, but apparently just not the one *I* love. In the middle of dinner, he broaches the topic of drugs, a non-sequitur to end all non-sequiturs given where we are. The conversation goes something like this:

"How's your steak?"

"I was thinking this weekend I'd go to the Roxy with Neal."

"Um, I was asking about your steak."

"I just wanted you to know. I know you always assume I do drugs when I go."

"So then you aren't going to do any?"

"I didn't say I wasn't."

My eyes mist over as I look out at the view of the city. I try not to let a single tear escape. I may not be able to control his drug use, regardless of how hard I try, but at least I can control my own display of emotion. As sad as I feel at this moment, I look at the city filled with infinite possibilities. Its strength and vitality reassure me everything will be okay. It reminds me I'm young and resilient. All conversation between us is over, my night is pretty much ruined, and the worst of it all is this heart-stopping view, unbeknownst to me, will never be the same again.

I always say enough is enough with him, but we always reunite after each of our many break-ups. But now, "enough" is supplanted by dearth. I have had enough nights of fighting about his drug use and a dearth of nights of enjoyment. The start of summer heralds the official end of our relationship. But that doesn't stop him from arriving at my house at two o'clock in the morning to try to convince me to take him back.

Two orbs of light climb the walls of my bedroom. This can only mean a car is pulling into my driveway. The moment those lights climb from the walls to the ceiling I can't help but think this can't be good. I leap out of bed to the window and find Drug-addled Ex's car is in the driveway. The engine stops. I run downstairs, turn off the house alarm, and open the door before he has a chance to ring the bell. Drug-addled Ex asks to come in, and I actually have to grant him entrance since I still live with my mother and don't want her to wake up because of him.

In my kitchen he tells me he can change. *Been there.*

He promises me he can stop with the drugs. *He can't.*

He beseeches me to take him back and is so utterly convinced things can work out that the following conversation ensues:

"If I go out and get an engagement ring and ask you to marry me right now, would that convince you to please take me back?"

In my head, I state, "God, no."

Out loud, I state, "God, no."

"Josh, this is killing me. I want to be with you. Why can't we be together? I'm not going to hurt you. Actually, I'm afraid to hurt you. Your mother will have me killed if I hurt you. She'd make a phone call and I'd be dead."

"You wouldn't be killed. You would just have both your legs broken."

"See, I can't tell when you're joking. You're so passive aggressive. And that's okay, just please let's get back together."

"It's late, can you go home? We are not getting back together."

Chapter Three: Summer of Love Redux

Breaking up with Drug-addled Boyfriend makes for a great time to take a trip to Las Vegas, hence, commence Summer 2001. Reveling in my emancipation, I fly to Las Vegas in order to let loose and let my inner child have the absolute blast he deserves. The remainder of the summer back home in New York equivocally enthralls me. Madonna's "Drowned World" tour, her first tour since 1993, guarantees me a great time at Madison Square Garden during the summer. What kind of gay would I be if I didn't like Madonna? People complain an awful lot about stereotypes, but no one ever says they aren't true. At least not if they are *my kind* of people. I'm kidding. (*No, I'm not.*)

Just when I come upon the Holy Grail of concerts, I come upon the Holy Grail of men. He's an aspiring writer, he's gorgeous, he lives in Brooklyn, and he is incredibly, jaw-droppingly bewitching. Mike charms me from the moment we meet in The Boiler Room in the East Village. I look behind me to see who he is smiling at and find no one is there.

"I'm smiling at you. There's no one behind you."

"I thought you were smiling at someone behind me so I didn't want to smile back since I figured that'd be awkward. I realize now you were smiling at me. This is definitely much more awkward."

Mike tries to stop himself from laughing and apologizes, "I'm sorry, I don't mean to laugh. That was cute. You're cute. What's your name?"

"Josh."

"I'm Mike. I'm here with a friend, but I couldn't help notice you over here. Who are you with? I saw you with someone and I don't want to overstep any boundaries. Specifically, I don't want a black eye. That guy looked big."

"Crafty of you, to wait till he goes to the bathroom. I like that. He's just a friend I'm with, actually my ex, John."

"Your ex-John, like you're a boy of the night, or your ex-boyfriend John? Either way, I'm intrigued."

"Very clever, I'll give you that. And I take the fifth."

"Thank you, I try. Can I get you a drink? You look like a… let me guess... Long Island?"

"Good guesser."

"Yes, I am. Wait, did you say good guesser or good kisser? Because I'm both."

"Smooth, very smooth. We'll get to that later if you play your cards right, mister Mike."

Over a couple of Midori Sours and Long Islands, we give each other a brief rundown of our personal histories to find we are both native New Yorkers, close with our mothers, employed, and single. We exchange phone numbers and, of course, the requisite kiss. He hasn't lied about being a good kisser, thankfully. We speak the next day and arrange to meet for a walk in the East Village.

On my way to meet him I can't help but wonder if I will like who and what I see when we meet. The dim lights of the Boiler Room, combined with the drinks I consumed, may have clouded my eyes and clouded a great many perceptions. I wonder how accurate my judgment could be given the circumstances. I spot his youthful countenance across the street, standing on the corner with his curly brown hair and big brown eyes, like a young lover eagerly awaiting his inamorato, ready to spring forth on his feet across the street that separates him from the object of his affection. I still can't believe he had been smiling at me and not at someone behind me. He walks up to me and moves his right arm from behind his back to present me with bunch of sunflowers. His craft knows no bounds, as he had asked me last night about my favorites, one of which included my favorite flower.

Drug-addled Ex may have been addicted to drugs, but drugs cannot, in any way, shape, or form, compare to the feeling this tender-hearted, well-versed, and highly educated man gives me when we spend time together. After a couple of dates, we go back to his place under the presupposition of hanging out. That presupposition turns out to be more like a premonition, as Mike does more than "hang out," he hangs out and then some, endowment-wise. I say a quick "Glory Be" in thanks of what the Good Lord has given, oh so bountifully, and wonder, but can things possibly get any better?

They can and do get better when we see each other on a frequent basis, pretty much about every other day. "Would you like to see the New York Philharmonic? They play on the Great Lawn in Central Park tomorrow at dusk. I can get some wine and cheese, and we can make a night of it under the stars," he asks. In for a penny, in for a pound I feel. He could ask me to walk in circles in front of Gray's Papaya with him and I would do it, but he consistently comes up with these ingenious New York centric ideas.

Situated in the middle of the great lawn, on a sheet with such a high thread count it would make Egyptian weavers writhe with awe, we listen to the Philharmonic and nibble on the goodies. Mike progresses from coyly touching my hand to kissing me, in the middle of the great lawn, with thousands of people around us. These thousands of people all melt away. Everything melts away, even the sounds of the Philharmonic become barely audible as I lose myself in the moment.

In an apologetic tone, Mike asks, "I'm sorry, Josh, I know it'll probably be lame but would you like to accompany me to a rooftop party on Friday night? We don't have to go, but it's work-related and I probably should go, but if you don't want to then we can definitely do something else."

Is he kidding? A rooftop party? I don't even try to keep my cool about it, but instead blurt out, "Rooftop party in Manhattan, with you? Have we met? Of course I'd love to."

Now that I have a rooftop party on the horizon, I take notice when I spot a sample sale while on my lunch break from work. I attempt to make my way to see the clothing but, as sample sales go, too many people vie for a deal and make it impossible for me to peruse for myself. I devise a plan of action to come back to the sample sale later, but before the after-work crowd. I cut my lunch drastically short and return to work immediately, so I can leave the office early today. At just about 4:15, I wish my co-workers a good weekend and let my feet carry me as swiftly as they can to the sample sale. I walk through the glass doors emblazoned with dozens of Xeroxed papers taped to them announcing the sale, and breathe a sigh of relief. Only a handful of people mill about the racks and boxes of clothing.

I locate the men's section, which is scant compared to the amount of room given to the women's section, and pillage for a bargain. These slacks are too small, and these are too big. These are the right size, but they don't do it for me. I spy a pair of men's pants on a hanger hanging from a nail in the wall, above the racks of clothing. A mirage, perhaps? The lights practically bounce off the pants from the sheen of the silvery grey fabric. Those would be perfect with black shoes and a black button down shirt, of which I have plenty. I glide over to the pants on the wall, pulled by some electro-chemical force. The tag indicates my size, 33. Surely, the pants have a hole in them somewhere. They cannot be perfect. I inspect them until someone surprises me at my side. She has seemingly appeared out of nowhere.

"Can I help you?" the girl asks.

"Sure, would you mind getting those pants down for me? Wow, that sounds so wrong. The ones on the wall, you know what I mean."

"Well," the girl responds, "that's a first, but yes, I can get those pants down for you, that's not a problem."

"I'm not even going to comment on that. Thank you so much."

Once the pants are down, off the wall that is, I check to see if they are damaged, defective, or the like. The girl reveals these clothes have never been worn by anyone, not even by models. These are the prototypes, made from better materials than those that will be used in the actual clothing lines. She brings me the perfect shirt for these pants. It's black, button-down, and divinity on a hanger. Although I don't need another black shirt, I succumb. My outfit complete, thoughts of the rooftop party permeate my consciousness and have me on cloud nine all the way home where I will change and prepare for the night ahead.

At the party, I make my way between the well-dressed men and women, and the impeccably outfitted servers with the little white towels draped so neatly over their right forearms, over to Mike. The austerity of this party already quickens my heart rate as I look around and find I'm an outsider about to be discovered where he doesn't belong. The moment I get to Mike though, all normalcy returns. The beaming, welcoming smile along with the kiss he plants on my lips calms my heartbeat as he whispers into my ear, "You are the hottest person in here." Surely, he has not seen his reflection lately. Dorian Gray would be jealous.

"You found the place all right I hope?" he asks.

"Definitely. You give really good directions, from landmarks to bodegas, there was no way I wouldn't find it."

"That's because if you didn't make it here my night would have been ruined. I really look forward to seeing you. A lot. I hope you know that."

"You have to stop being so sweet. And so handsome. You make me sweat I get so nervous and self-conscious."

"You get nervous around me? That's adorable."

"Umm… it's gross, actually," I reply as I wipe the back of my neck with my hand.

"Adorable. And what do you have to be self-conscious about?"

"I…"

"Nothing," he interrupts, "nothing is what you have to be self-conscious about. Let me repeat myself. You," he grazes my lips with his, "have nothing to be," he lands a tender kiss, "self-conscious about," he kisses me deeply with his eyes open as he looks into mine.

While lying in bed after the rooftop party, Mike broaches the topic of boyfriend-dom. As enamored with Mike as I have become, I can't help but think of how great a time I'm having with things just the way they are, without labels, without the impending sense of doom my last relationship heralded. I'm neither seeing anyone else, nor interested in seeing anyone else, except for maybe myself. Not ready to take a lesser part in my own life in order to become part of a couple once again, so quickly after the termination of my relationship with Drug-addled Ex, I let Mike know that being boyfriends, just the term alone, is something I can't handle at this time. Mike, however, doesn't want to settle for less. And just like that, single Josh is once again unleashed on the dating scene in New York.

Two weeks later, I go to G Lounge for a drink before I head home for the night. While out, I meet a potential love interest named Steven. He works in the same field as I, is about the same age as I, and is also a BBQ boy. In other words, he is a Brooklyn, Bronx, or Queens boy, born and raised. We hit it off from the moment he, while wearing a watch, asks, "Pardon me, do you have the time?"

Perplexed at the fact that someone in this day and age says 'pardon me' in a gay bar, I respond, "Sure, it's eleven thirty."

"Thank you much."

The guy is so scruffily good looking that animal magnetism forces me to continue the conversation in some way.

As if I don't know the area, I ask, "Are there any other good bars around here?"

"I'm not really sure. This seems to be the popular one. I don't typically go out often, but it was so nice out I figured why not."

"I'm glad you did. I could've stood here all night and not have spoken to anyone. People seem so timid about approaching others. So, definitely glad you came out tonight."

"Truth be told, I ummm, well I didn't need the time. See?" He points to the watch on his wrist. "I just wanted to talk to you. Corny, right?"

"No, not corny at all. It's not like you pretended not to know the area or anything, just to keep a conversation going."

"Hmm... I thought you seemed like a native. I was like, 'Why's he asking me what the good places are around here?' Hey, feel like taking a walk, since it's nice out? We can talk easier that way too."

"Sounds great to me."

When we leave the bar, we walk from Chelsea (never one to break a stereotype) to Bryant Park and sit on the steps at the park and talk about what keeps us entertained and busy in the city until three a.m. The morning will arrive regardless but, for the time being, we find ourselves enveloped in conversation and the brewing sentiments of affection.

* * *

From: Josh
To: Steven
Sent: 8/29/01
Subject: Good afternoon :0)

Hey Handsome,

Thought I'd drop you a line to say hello. Hope you had a nice morning. Great, to be honest, now I'm wondering where the term "drop a line" came from. I know what "do a line" means (Whitney Houston's remixes are awesome by the way) but I'm not too sure what "drop a line" means. I imagine it's like when you are a kid in a tree house and you write a letter and put it on the hook of a fishing pole and drop the letter down to the person below, hence dropping a line. Sidenote, I grew up in Bensonhurst so no tree houses for me. Regardless, that's how I'm imagining it :0)

Attached is a pdf I received from a website that sends out useful info to people in sales. Most of it is common sense stuff, but the kind you don't really think about until someone brings it to your attention. (If that makes sense to you.) Anyway, when you have a second, you can read it. It's applicable to everyday life too.

Enough shop talk. Decide what you are doing for lunch yet? I'm not really hungry, so I guess I'll have to play it by ear. I can go to the WTC and shop around inside. I can pop into Century 21, too, if time permits. I'll probably go to the seaport though. It's nice out, so it's probably better to stay outdoors and get some fresh air.

Till later,
Josh

Going Down and Moving On

From: Steven
To: Josh
Sent: 8/29/01
Subject: Re: Good afternoon :0)

Right back at ya' Gorgeous,

My morning was indeed pleasurable, especially
since you just put a smile on my face by appearing in
my email. Aside from your email though, not too
much has been going on. Thank you for the website
info too, there's a certain je ne se qua (I sound fancy)
to having a reminder about best practices. If you want
the plant to grow, you have to water it, right? Hope
you've been having at least an equally pleasurable
morning.

I just got back from lunch. I went for
souvlaki with a side order of baba ganouche.
Was feeling like I should get myself out of the
box, so to speak. Gotta love street-stand food,
it's one of New York's bountiful treasures. I'm
just keeping my fingers crossed that I don't get
sick from it. The double-edged sword of street
stand food is that when it's good it's great, but
when it's not good, well, watch out.

It was a most relaxing lunch hour. I dined (okay, I
ate) at a little spot by work where there's a fountain of
sorts. It's quite a relaxing place to have lunch or take a
break from work. I always love the fact that water can
really touch your inner being. You must have a complete

---

blast with your office being walking distance from the South Street Seaport and the WTC. You have the best of both worlds there.

So, ummm, I was wondering if you would be amenable to doing something tomorrow. I don't know if you have any plans, but I know I'd like to be involved in the creation of some with you. I'm going to earn superhero status while I wait to receive your response. Seriously though, let me know if you can meet up tomorrow, we can devise a plan. Maybe we can grab dinner at Yaffa Café or something like that. I'd even be open to something more commercial like the Fashion Cafe but they closed down, which is odd considering how they charged twenty bucks for an empty plate served with a small glass of water. Go figure.

Be well and talk soon.
Steven

* * *

I have a better encounter with Steven on the first night we meet than I had on any of the times I went out with Drug-addled Ex. And it can't be attributed to the butterfly feeling I get in my stomach when I start going out with someone new. Because I didn't even have that feeling when I started to go out with Drug-addled Ex. It was as if the butterflies knew, in that instance, they would have been better off staying in their cocoons and cutting their losses. If only I had done the same. This new encounter with Steven, though, really intrigues me. The butterflies rightfully spread their wings and flutter about my insides. I think, hey, I can completely get used to this. I readily take Steven up on his offer to go out for dinner.

We meet up, after work, in the East Village at the Yaffa Café for dinner. The hostess leads us out to the back courtyard area where we take seats among the luscious flowers and plants. We jump into conversation before the menus are even placed in front of us.

I inquire, "So how long have you been working at your current job?"

"A little over two years."

"Nice. Where did you go to school?"

"Hunter College."

"I know you live in Queens, where's your family?"

"My mom and dad live nearby, not too far. I just felt it was time to get out on my own."

"What's your background? Irish?"

"Yes."

"Do you have any siblings?"

"No, I'm the only child. I feel like I'm being interviewed. Wow, you ask a lot of questions. Actually, I guess this is an interview. Aren't all first dates interviews?"

"I'm sorry, it's a bad habit of mine. There's always so much about a person I want to know. Your turn, ask me anything. And you're right, first dates are pretty much interviews. I should be a headhunter." Immediately reddening in embarrassment, I try to clarify, "I mean I ask a lot of questions on a first date, so it would be natural for me to be a headhunter like for a job." I quickly shake my head and say, "For a job-job, not a," I whisper, "blowjob." I take a breath, sit back and confess, "Foot in mouth and we barely opened our menus."

"Don't be sorry, you have a good style. No nonsense yet honestly disarming. I can appreciate that."

"Wait till you see what I ask you when dessert arrives. I'm kidding, totally kidding."

"We'll have to see, I wouldn't be surprised," Steven chuckles. "So, you're from Brooklyn. Where's your family originally from?"

"Brooklyn."

"No, I mean before that."

"Like my ancestors? My grandparents came from Italy."

"You're not Irish?"

"Nope. I'm Italian."

"You don't have any Irish in you at all?"

With an arched eyebrow, I respond, "Not yet."

"I would have bet you…" Steven pauses mid-sentence, waits a few seconds, blushes, and smiles ear to ear. "I just got that," he admits. "You're fast."

"Hey, that's what it says in my high school yearbook! Kidding, totally kidding," I respond, and follow it up with a quick shake of my head back and forth as I fake whisper, "I'm not kidding."

"You're bad," Steven plays, "and I kind of like it."

* * *

From: Josh
To: Steven
Sent: 08/31/09
Subject: Hey there sexy dangerous :0)

Well, I had a totally great night. Enjoyed every minute of it (you know that) but I just wanted to say it again anyway. And you were a complete gentleman, too cute. Hope you got in on time. My train ride this morning was a quick one.

I even had time to go to the chiropractor. I always feel that when he goes to crack my neck like it might be the last thing that happens to me. It's like I know he's a chiropractor and he's been trained and all, but it's still his job. And well, let's face it, everyone slips up at their job at one time or another. He tells me, "I'm going to crack your neck now." And I'm like, "ut-oh." The funniest was about a month ago, when I went to him on the same day I was going to go to the Madonna concert at MSG. Well, that's when I thought, Okay, God, if he slips up today this will not be funny. I figured that would really suck because I'd never seen Madonna live before, and being dead, well that's not so cool a thing in itself either.

Already finished breakfast (fiesta bagel with fat free cream cheese). "Fiesta" bagel, kind of a glorified name for a vegetable bagel. Never really had one before, it was good though. Also just got an email from human resources. The office closes at 3 today, which is good, no complaints. But since I'm meeting my friend Vinny at 7, that leaves a lot of down-time. What to do, what to do.

So I hope your morning is going well, getting a lot of reading done I would assume. I know, I know, don't assume (the whole Felix Unger thing-- you know what I'm talking about, right?) I'm sure you do.

Anywhoo, I'm going to bring this lengthy letter to a close with a big MWAH :0)

Till later,
Josh

* * *

From: Steven
To: Josh
Sent: 8/31/01
Subject: RE: hey there sexy dangerous

Grrrrr .... Sexy and Dangerous don't you forget it.
     Color me stoked that you had a good night, I can't be happier. When I go to the museum I like to take my time and enjoy all of the facets of a work. I'd definitely like to see you more and get to know you better. Considering the night we had I somehow still managed to get to work on time. It's beyond difficult for me, under normal circumstances, to get to work on time. Today though, a Friday no less, I'm on time. You must have put a spring in my step. Be proud grasshopper, because that's not an easy feat, or should I say feet? Ba dump bump.

Steven

* * *

From: Steven
To: Josh
Sent: 9/5/01
Subject: Good afternoon :0)

Hey Gorgeous,
     So even though today was doing a good job at going by pretty fast, it has decided to pretend it's in a union and invoke a slow-down. Good grief. Alas, the day continues at an unfortunately glacial pace. I hope your day is not moving so…
slllloooooo…..wwwwww…..lllly.

Be well and talk soon,
Steven

* * *

From: Steven
To: Josh
Sent: 9/6/01
Subject: Re: Good afternoon :0)

Greetings and Salutations,
A second cup of coffee, okay a third cup of coffee, was giving me palpitations. Grrrr. So then I decided to drink a lot of water to dilute the coffee that was in me. Now I can't sit at my desk for more than oh about eight minutes without having to get up to pee. Double grrr. Ho-hum, I still have a bunch of things to do today including, but not limited to, making additional media kits for the salespeople, (boring), reviewing our competition (yaay), update accounts receivable (double boring), check my other email account (double yaay), Talk to Josh later tonight (an occasion of infinite pleasure).

Be well and talk soon,
Steven

* * *

Elation. Elation is the only word suited to describe what it feels like when someone refers to talking to me as a task of "infinite pleasure." I think I even exhale. As for my other friends, John plans a trip to Vegas for Labor Day and it is that kind of celebratory time in the lives of young twenty-something New Yorkers. Unfortunately, the time for celebration in the lives of New Yorkers is about to come to a dramatic close.

* * *

From: John
To: Josh
Sent: 09/10/01
Subject: Hi Josh

Hi Josh,

What have you been up to lately? Long time, no see. Just got back from Las Vegas. I really wish you would have come, especially since we haven't ever gone away together. I know, coming from New York, summer temperatures in Las Vegas shouldn't be so bad, but holy cow was it scorching hot there. And I thought, when you live in New York, everywhere else in comparison would be cheap. Not the case though. The buffets were to die for. Josh, talk about gluttony: we completely indulged every single night at the buffets. I'm so glad we don't have those buffets here, I would never do anything else. I also got addicted to an amazing club across from the Hard Rock Hotel.

It's nice to be back home though. That heat was unbearable. I sweat so much that every time I changed my shirt I looked at the back of it like a Rorshach test and tried to figure out what the sweat mark resembled. At least autumn is right around the corner. I know it sounds crazy but I'm already wearing boots. Don't worry, they aren't hardcore winter boots, they're more fashionable ones. I'm aware it's not the season yet, I just want winter to be here already.

And speaking of moving on, I should ask you for help. I haven't even decorated my living room yet and I've been there a year. You're the photographer, do you have anything that I can have enlarged, framed, and hung up? What did you wind up doing over Labor Day weekend? I imagine you had a great time whatever you did. You always seem to have fun regardless of what you do. That's pretty impressive.
Okay, I should try to get some work done.

Talk soon and have a good week,
John

* * *

From: Josh
To: John
Sent: 9/10/01
Subject: Re: Hi Josh

Hey John :0)

Glad to hear you had a good time, you deserve the best :0) I went to see De La Guarda on Labor Day

Weekend. They re-did it, so at least it was a little different.

I'm going bowling at Bowlmor Lanes (it's right near Union Square) today after work at about 6:00. Steven's going to come. I'll tell you about him on the phone, all good stuff. He's going to try to get some friends to go and so am I. If you can, I'd love for you to come. I haven't seen you in months.

Let me know either way, hopefully you can come. Bring your boyfriend, of course, if he's interested :0) And regarding the photography, honestly, I got caught up on the word "hung." Good God I am so immature sometimes. But of course I'd love to help, that's awesome that you thought of me.

Till later,
Josh

* * *

De La Guarda, an interactive show in Union Square, involves flying Argentines, pounding music, hands in the air, and feet off the floor, and it captures the vivacity of the summer of 2001. The show exudes energy and causes jaws to drop, much like New York City itself. John's statement about how I make the best out of any situation rings true. Nothing happens so bad it becomes irreparable.

On the night of September 10th, I plan to go bowling with Steven, but, since none of our friends exhibit interest in bowling, Steven and I decide to do something more intimate, just the two of us. We share s'mores at Cosi and then to the Quad Cinema on West 13th Street between 5th Avenue and Avenue of the Americas. It is the quintessential New York date. Drug-addled Ex has completely phased out of the picture and a couple of months in the life of a gay is the equivalent of... I'm bad at math. Regardless, let it be clear that the gays, at least the New York ones, bounce back rather quickly from break-ups. I could try to get existential and postulate the reason for this lies in the sub-culture's tangential obsession with appearance and age, but I can't type all that, it will ruin my manicure.

The date consists of witty conversation, good food, city atmosphere, a visit to an independent movie theater to see *All Over the Guy* with New York favorite Christina Ricci, and a surprise torrential rainstorm when the film lets out. I enjoy being caught in the occasional torrential downpour because it is few and far between I can be so engulfed in something so natural.

It's rare to concede to being so overpowered by something but therein lay the allure. It's akin to going for a massage. I was brought up with the admonishment I should avoid talking to strangers. If someone stands too close to me on a subway train, or sits too close to me in a movie theater, I roll my eyes, exhale sharply, and ask myself how this relative stranger could have the audacity to invade my personal space. And sometimes I even go so far as to ask this aloud. I use the term "relative stranger" loosely, as it has always eluded me how someone could be both relative and stranger at the same time. But, I digress. Taking this into consideration, getting massaged by someone, a stranger, a paid stranger at that, should have me recoiling at the thought of his or her touch. But I don't. Instead, like I do with this rainstorm, I give in and let myself enjoy the freedom that comes with letting go.

We see the eight-twenty p.m. showing, so by the time the movie lets out and we make our way to the corner of Avenue of the Americas we are completely soaked, down to the underwear. It's all right though, as it's all part of letting go.

We take shelter under the awning of the Cosi where we met at the start of the night. Pressed with our backs against the glass windows of the Cosi, the rain patters against our bodies. The streetlights illuminate the pearl-sized globes of rain that relentlessly stream down. I brush a droplet of rain from Steven's brow with my thumb, trace the right side of his face, cup his chin with my fingertips, and gently motion him forward for a light kiss.

Splashing sounds interrupt our kiss. Two girls run across from the west side of the street to the east side when the flood of water that surges south along the gutter pulls off one girl's flip-flop. It shimmies between the parked cars and the curb, caught in the rush of water that continues to fall. The footwear propels past another car while the girl's friend offers, through laughter, "It's over there, it's over there." She points at the car's back tire where it wedges itself. Cue the girl's high-pitched squeal of "My shoe!" She lurches forward and reaches out to reclaim her footwear when lightning obliterates the darkness and a clap of thunder startles her upright. The moment to claim her flip-flop passes as the footwear leaps from its wedged position between car tire and curb and lands on the sidewalk. Bewildered but relieved, she exclaims, "Gotcha!" and snatches her possession.

Oh, New York. It really makes for the perfect, absolute quintessential, New York night. As for what tomorrow brings, who knows. Absorbed in this night, the date, the s'mores, the movie, and the rainstorm, tomorrow doesn't exist. It's all about tonight. And no matter what may come, September 10th will always be Old New York to me.

Chapter Four: A Not-so-Good Mo(u)rning

The red numbers on the digital clock that sits on my desk read 8:45 a.m. as I settle myself into work. I check my emails and pass by the fax machine to see if any faxes have come through overnight when I hear a co-worker bluster on in an odd, excited, and high-pitched manner. I wonder what has gotten into him this morning, as he is never usually this animated. Actually, he is never animated at all. When I hear what he says, I have to wonder if he is joking. He speaks and at the same time he laughs at the absurdity of what he says.

That's such a weird thing for him to say, that a plane just flew into the north tower of the World Trade Center. He continues as his hands fly in the air, further giving life to his words, "What was the pilot thinking, how could someone fly a plane into the World Trade Center? What, did he just learn to fly? How could he not see it? Look out the window. If you look from Ryan's office you can see people jumping out of the Trade Center. Go look." My only thought is, why is he saying this? It definitely can't be true. A general fluster in the office ensues during which staff members realize he may be serious. Several people walk to the windows, some make their way at a quicker pace than others. I put the phone receiver down on its cradle, instead of dialing in to check my voicemails, and walk over to the windows. My coworker, apparently, has been telling the truth.

A plane has undeniably flown directly into one of the towers of the Trade Center. A girl from the accounting department lifts a phone receiver off its cradle near the row of windows facing the Twin Towers and dials someone. I pass Ryan's office and find Ryan stands behind his desk as he looks out his window toward the Twin Towers. He borders on disbelief. He merely borders on disbelief because his usual arrogance still remains which makes him think he can handle anything and everything that comes his way, and by handle I mean delegate. Like a scene out of *Working Girl*, the undeserving and pompous miscreant has the plush office with a view, while the well-intentioned, hard-working underling functions from a cubicle.

He invites me to come into his office, to come closer, take a look, and watch the people as they jump from the tower. Yes, he actually makes it sound as if it is a bunch of circus freaks I am about to witness do an act. I see the tower in question loom behind Ryan and I know if I look directly at it I will never be able to forget the image of the people who plunge to their deaths. At first, I don't look directly at it but I see it in my periphery. And then I take a look because I feel I have to take at least a quick look, and I swear I see two people jump from up high, and soar down while they hold hands with each other. I look away but I can still see the towers, the fire, and the smoke. What on earth is happening?

I return to my desk to call my mom to let her know I'm okay but, as I dial, I look at the digital clock and realize it's still too early to call her. I hang up the phone. She's not at work yet. My train, depending on which route I take to work, lets me out under the Towers, and I don't want her to worry that I am caught in the heart of the commotion. Today, the B train arrived first. If the M train had arrived first, I would have been under the Trade Center and wound up going to the Century 21 to do some quick underwear shopping. If I left home a minute or so earlier or later, my story would be quite different, if I had one to tell at all.

Should I call Steven? I can let him know I'm okay. No, he's not there either. I go back to the windows where most of the staff members have gathered. I wonder, where is my friend Phoebe? I do a quick lap around the office to look for her, but I don't find her. Evidently, it's back to the windows for me.

Charlie Casso

The girl holds the phone receiver in her trembling hand and, while she bawls, still manages to narrate what she sees to the person on the other end of the telephone. Someone at the window states, "I wish I had a camera," and it snaps me to my reality that I always carry a camera on me, with extra film, too, since I never know what I'll see in New York. I run to my cubicle, open my messenger bag, grab my camera, and head back to take a few shots of the Tower on fire as the smoke billows out from it. Sometimes, from behind the lens, I can take myself out of reality for a bit. When I watch people or events through the camera lens, I become a mere observer in lieu of a participant. In this case, I definitely need my camera to remove me from my reality.

The girl's voice rises through her tears as she screams into the telephone receiver, "Oh my God, here comes another plane it's going to hit the..." She cannot finish her exclamation, as she is cut off by a bellowing one-word scream: "RUN!" "Run" is screamed from the crowd as a second plane makes direct contact with the south tower, causing smoke, debris, and fire to rush from the tower. The windows where we stand wham loudly in their panes as our building jolts severely. My boss, Lynette, runs alongside as she pulls people by their arms, shoulders, waists, whatever she can grab, and makes them move along with her. Lynette directs me, "Get what you need. Let's go. OUT. We need to leave. Josh, stay away from any windows, the building might collapse."

I snatch my messenger bag off my desk, throw it on, pick up the phone, and dial the number of the bank where my mom works in Brooklyn. I notice the red light on my phone indicates voicemail awaits me, but I have no time for that now. A co-worker of my mom's answers the phone and immediately gives the receiver to my mom when she hears it's me. I am quite certain my mom has told everyone at work how close my workplace is to the Trade Center and to give her the phone immediately when I call. I'm also certain she's tried calling me several times but has not received a response as I've been all over the office. I tell her I'm heading home, I will see her soon, and I love her. I quickly toss the receiver to its place and run to catch up to Lynette. A bunch of us pile into the elevator to escape the building.

Now I know I just talked to my mom, and as any mom would attest, getting into an elevator in a shaking building is not a good idea. One should always use the stairs in such an instance. In my defense though, who could really think clearly at this moment? All common sense, actually all sense for that matter, cannot be taken for granted at moments such as these. The elevator works, although once we are in it we realize we might not have made a good decision getting in. "Should we be in here?" I ask as the elevator rocks from side to side. Say a quick prayer and try not to hyperventilate, because every moment and bit of help is necessary at this point. "Ding," everyone races off the elevator, through the lobby, and out of the building. Now what? It's barely ten minutes past nine.

Chapter Five: Outdoors, Where It's safe?

Phoebe runs out of the building and asks, "What's this all about?"

"Two planes just struck the Twin Towers. I don't know what's going on, but it's not good," I reply. "Where were you? I was worried when I couldn't find you."

"I was in the bathroom. I thought I felt something but I was, well, I was on the toilet and I thought it was me," she confesses. "I knew something was wrong when I got off the train, I saw everyone looking up and all, there was a weird vibe in the air, but I didn't want to get here late."

"I don't know how I missed the first hit. Wait, I do know! I was walking past the kitchen and I heard a really loud noise but I just thought someone was breaking ice on the sink or something. I thought that was really loud."

"The building didn't shake?"

"I think it did. I was walking though, so I guess I just didn't feel it."

"This can't be an accident. One plane, okay, an accident. A stupid one, but an accident. Two? This is intentional. Something bad is going on, Josh."

"We should leave. Let's get home. Do you want to come with me out of the city?" I ask.

"It's smart to get out but I also don't want to be trapped out of my home if I leave and we aren't allowed back in. I'd better hightail it home myself. Worse comes to worse, I can walk."

Shannon, runs out of the building, grabs me, and directs, "Josh, we need to make our way to Brooklyn." On that note, Phoebe and I embrace as only the best of friends can, and promise each other that we will be all right.

Shannon takes my hand as we leave the outside of our office building and head to the trains. I should have said to the mass confusion. Trains? What trains? People run in every direction, this way and that. But where are the trains? People who head away from the train platforms say there are no trains, to get out of the train station and go above ground. The panic-stricken looks on their faces indicate they indeed tell the truth, the very ugly truth. Without train service to get us out of here, we will be stuck in this area for a while. Shannon and I turn around and start to make our way back out of the train station.

On the way out, we try to tell the people who head in there are no trains. We don't try to stop people on a one-on-one basis or anything so futile. Rather, we just yell "no trains" and "turn around the trains aren't running" so hopefully they won't waste their time in this confusion waiting for a train which will never come. Most of the people we try to warn barely pay us any mind at all. They move in a daze, in shock. I can't blame them. The police also try to warn people now not to use the trains. We must have missed the last train.

Charlie Casso

Once again, Shannon and I find ourselves on Fulton Street where we started. I wonder how we will escape the city. Shannon suggests we go over the Brooklyn Bridge. I must admit, and anyone who knows me can attest to this fact, I am geographically challenged. I tend to think I can navigate myself around New York City though, so I figure we can make it home by foot. It's our only option.

Around Cedar Sinai we race, and I snap pictures along the way. A line of gurneys haunts the outside of the hospital, but no one lies in them. And nurses too, wait around. I would imagine the hospital would be filled with people. We are so close to what is happening that surely people need medical assistance.

As I look back, a woman right beside me wheels a carriage with her baby in it. The look on her face is unfortunately common this morning. The panic and dread smeared across the stranger's face brings me to tears because it makes all of my fears and anxiety surface. The questions "will we make it out of here?" and "is this the end?" are born this morning.

The traffic on the bridge, foot traffic this morning, is out of control. The bridge teems with more people than I have ever seen before. It's a mass exodus of the city. The entrance to the bridge wraps around the downtown streets but we are pretty close to it now. At least, I think we are close to it. I have never navigated myself from the downtown area by work over the Brooklyn Bridge before today. The enormity of walking towards the entrance to the bridge, and seeing just how many people will attempt to walk over the bridge, literally takes my breath away.

The WTC and the Brooklyn Bridge fill my eyes. Flames and smoke emanate from one, while I walk towards the other. I wonder if I will make it across the bridge. It's one of those "is this really going to happen?" moments I see coming but I don't know if I can handle or not. But I can do it. Actually, I have to do it. What is the other option? Snap.

Chapter Six: Crossing the Brooklyn Bridge (And Making the Sign of the Cross in Hopes We Don't Die on the Bridge)

Once Shannon and I make it onto the bridge, we are amongst scores of people who walk in the same direction. Men and women walk in front of us, in back of us, and surround us on all sides for as far as my eyes can see. I look behind me because I simply cannot believe the mass exodus of which I am a part. Under normal circumstances, being part of such a magnitude of people would make me completely lose my breath. Here though, now though, I don't have the luxury of time to think too much about anything. All I know is I just have to go. This is definitely not the time for weakness, hesitation, or contemplation.

As the bridge overflows with pedestrians, people spill over and walk in the car lanes. An emergency vehicle occasionally careens down the lanes into the city, but those are few and far between. The people who walk in the car lanes get directed to use the footpath, so they climb up and hoist themselves over the fence. I'm sure it is a lot safer for them this way, out of the reach of the sporadic, speeding vehicle.

There is one bicyclist I notice who heads into the city in a car lane. A large paparazzi-type camera hangs from a thick black strap on his chest. Aside from him, I don't notice others head into the city over the Brooklyn Bridge. Smoke and fire emanate from the towers.

What is happening? Why is that noise so close? The clear, unmistakable sound of an airplane descends upon me at a speed beyond reproach. The roar deafens and frightens us all. A collective scream rolls like thunder from one end of the bridge to the other. People hit the ground as they throw their hands in the air to protect their heads. The bridge quakes from the proximity of the plane, but the plane swoops right past the bridge, leaving it to rock in its wake. The relieved mass gets back on its feet, slowly pulls hands down from over heads, past frightened faces. I exhale for now, because an Air Force plane, one of our own planes, soars above and I remain alive. Back on my feet, still standing, I resume my walk across the bridge. Shannon directs me to look to the left where I see something I don't recognize. I see the streets below, but the sidewalks don't look right at all. It's hard to make out from here, but they don't look like sidewalks. Alongside the buildings there appears to be what looks like darkly colored confetti, just a bunch of different colored specks on the ground.

"What is that?" I ask.

Shannon's response whelms me. "It's people," she states.

It is a colossal mass of people who, like us, attempt to make their way out of the city.

The people in front of me walk along, just as confused and scared as everyone else. Some cry, and rightfully so. Others try to use their cell phones while they walk, but for most this is a useless endeavor. Cell phone calls do not go through. Is it the sheer magnitude of calls being attempted at this time that's blocking them from going through? Or is this the end? I'm not sure.

The young woman on my right sobs hysterically while she tries to get a phone call to go through. Shannon attempts to console her.

"Sweetie," Shannon addresses the woman, "you're going to make it. We are all going to make it."

The woman blurts out, through tears, "I can't get my dad on the phone. He's in there and I can't get him on the phone." The woman attempts to turn around toward the city again.

Shannon takes the woman's hand in hers and directs her to Brooklyn once more. "He will be fine. Listen to me," she says as she looks into the girl's eyes, "I'm sure he's out by now. You need to stay strong and get yourself to the other side of this bridge."

"No, I'm going back. I need to find him, I need to find my dad," she says as she turns back around and attempts to dart through the onslaught of pedestrians.

Shannon grabs her once again, "They won't let you through. Please, listen to me. The police, the firemen, no one will let you into the building. It's too late. We have to get across the bridge."

"I'm going. I have to find my dad. I'll get in, they'll have to let me in," marks the last thing she says as she breaks free from Shannon and scurries through the crowd back into the unknown.

"That woman," Shannon qualms, "she'll never make it."

"Shannon," I say, "you tried, that's all you could do. You tried." I look back to see if I can see the woman in the crowd, but she has disappeared amongst the masses.

I trip and nearly turn my ankle over God knows what. Please let it not be a person. I look down. Oh. My. God. High heels cover almost every square inch of the bridge. Those who wear heels while they hightail it for their lives kick them off when they realize they can go faster without them. Either that, or their feet just hurt too much from walking in heels. Something finally makes sense to me, even if it is as simple as why the bridge is littered with high heels. As I snap a picture of the mass of people in front of me, I trip once more. I realize the picture will come out weird, either blurry or off-center.

I raise my camera to take another picture, to replace the previous one I'm sure will turn out crude when developed. As I depress the shutter button the second time, something odd happens. I hear crumbling. Can crumbling be a sound? It sounds like a thunderous crumbling with loud cracks. It sounds as if God's back is being broken.

Hypersensitive to sounds and anything else that can signal something bad, everyone turns the moment a sign of danger nears. So, the people closer to the Manhattan side of the bridge, like me, turn immediately to see what makes the crumbling, cracking noise. The sound signals the collapse of many things, primarily the collapse of the South Tower of the World Trade Center.

Stay behind the lens, I tell myself. Just stay behind the lens. That is how I will live through this. As I stay behind the lens I run for my life, as does everyone else, because instinct says to run.

Charlie Casso

Charlie Casso

Maybe it isn't really happening. I run alongside Shannon for the duration of the collapse of the South Tower, and turn back every few seconds to make sure the bridge isn't collapsing behind me. I snap a picture each time I turn back as well. Shannon and I take a moment to stop and catch our breath right past the middle of the bridge. Now on the Brooklyn side, I am compelled to look back at the city. And I do. I place my hands on a guardrail facing the city and absorb the remains.

A mess of smoke is all that can be seen where the Twin Towers had only hours ago stood. I realize the city I know and love has been changed entirely and will never be the same. Neither will I. I lean on the guardrail and, over the edge of the bridge, burst out in tears. For the moment, it is uncontrollable, a bloodletting of sorts. Tears pour from me. The brevity of the situation hits me in a moment of clarity. Things will never be the same, and I just let it out. Suddenly, Shannon grabs my shoulders and quite forcibly shakes some of my senses back into me. She urges, "Josh, let's go. Get it together. Come on, Josh, we have to go, this isn't safe." I wipe my tears with the backs of my trembling hands. Still standing there, for one moment more, I look back at the city that will never be the same.

The Brooklyn Bridge lets us out in Downtown Brooklyn. It's amazing how instincts can really guide a person in a time of need. Using our combined instincts, Shannon and I make it from the name streets in Brooklyn, which can be quite confusing to navigate, to the numbered streets and avenues. Along the way, people already sport masks over their faces to help them breathe without swallowing the ash that floats in the air.

The most disturbing of all on the Brooklyn side, the part that hits me most, is a mother who walks alongside her children, all of whom wear face masks.

The buses run, but they teem with people. Hordes of passengers cluster in the stairwells, pressed against each other and the glass of the doors. The bus drivers do not mind it in this instance, on this day. Priorities have shifted and it is time we protect ourselves as well as strangers. At 5th avenue and 69th street in Brooklyn, Shannon and I board a bus that has a bit of space. It carries Shannon home to 13th Avenue and me to my 86th street stop. My phone chimes in my pocket.

"Hello?" I ask, curious to know if there will really be a connection.

"Josh, it's John. Are you okay?"

"I'm heading home. Are you okay?"

"I'm fine. I was worried about you because I know where you work. Make sure you get home and call me if you need anything."

"Will do. I haven't been able to make or get any calls today. I'll try my mom so I can let her know I'm headed home."

I call my mom and find she is home already, and she awaits my arrival. When I get off of the bus I stop at the express photo shop. A compulsion drives me to get the pictures developed. I need to see what I just went through. As advertised in the store's window, I have the photographs in my hands within minutes. I take the pictures in hand and head right home. When I get to my corner, I see my mom stands outside on the porch. As soon as I see her, I run down the block, up the stairs, and into her arms. I'm home.

Chapter Seven: Reality Used to Be a Friend of Mine; Now It Haunts My Sleep

Let the nightmares begin. The first night, September 11th, I dream a dream. I sleep, snuggled in my bed, fluffy blue pillow under my head, my body on its side. Then, crash, a helicopter smashes through my bedroom window, blades first, chopping through the bricks, sending shards of glass and concrete through the night air. I pull the covers over me to protect me, but the chopper comes right at me, the weight of it threatens to flatten me while its rotors chop me to slivers. Drenched in sweat, I jolt out of sleep, and gasp for air. My heart races. I survey my room, completely horrified.

I attempt sleep once more. Suddenly, I'm walking underground in a subway station. I pass the huge advertisements plastered on the walls, faster and faster, but the station doesn't seem to have an exit. Finally, a break in the wall appears. I bound up the concrete steps by twos and threes until I reach greyish daylight. As I'm leaping to the top step, shards of brick rain down from above. I cover my head with my hands and hit the ground as an airplane ricochets off of the building and careens down toward the subway entrance. I awaken with the covers pulled so tight over me that I can't breathe. I fall out of bed onto the floor and shake the remainder of the covers off of me.

I do nothing. My mind is a blank. I don't put the television on because I can't bear to watch the news reports as I'm sure they constantly rehash the events. It's one of those sitting on the floor while pulling the light string over and over, making the light go on and off, moments. Except I don't have a light like that. Plus, I don't like sitting on the floor; it hurts my ass. So I lie on my bed until the ring of my telephone interrupts the silence.

"Hey, it's me."

"Hey, Steven."

"I was going to come over and surprise you."

"That would've been an awesome surprise."

"Good, I'm glad you think so, because I'm a few blocks away. I wanted to make sure I gave you at least a little notice."

"Nice! I'm here, come on over."

"Be right there."

Steven's inter-borough visit displays incredible thoughtfulness on his part. I know the trip from Queens to Brooklyn takes a while, especially with the trains as messed up as they are now. It's September twelfth. He brings a couple of desserts I like from the bakery near his apartment. They're like two big round shortbread cookie things with raspberry jelly in the middle. A cookie sandwich, covered in confectioners' sugar. I get distracted by all things sweet, so Steven and the desserts suit me well. Steven is by my side, considerate enough to be with me when I need him the most. We take a stroll to a deli near my house where we purchase breakfast sandwiches and orange juice and take them to the shore. We sit on a bench, most of which are vacant, look out at the water, talk, and reflect. We agree about how things seem so different so suddenly. We don't really say too much though, we still remain in shock. At the shore, we soak in a comfortingly uncomfortable silence.

Steven returns home to Queens and, that evening, I arrange to go for dinner with John at L&B Spumoni Gardens in Bensonhurst. On our way to dinner, a report comes on the radio that Whitney Houston has died of a drug overdose. The report states she was taken to the hospital because her heart stopped. John expresses his deep concern about the death of Whitney and, as most gay men are apt to do, he clutches at his own chest and exclaims, "Oh my God, not Whitney."

Cue my first outburst, "Are you serious? Innocent people are dead and families are suffering, and you're upset over Whitney overdosing? There's something wrong with you." As it turns out, Whitney was in the hospital, her heart did supposedly stop, but with everything else going on the story gets dropped like a hot, crack-is-whack potato. Ironically, a re-release of the single of Whitney's Star Spangled Banner is issued. Additionally, Mariah Carey's movie *Glitter* prepares to open nationwide. I am one of five people, and that includes John, who attend a showing at the Marlboro Theater in Brooklyn. What a very sad state of affairs.

* * *

From: Ryan
To: All
Sent: 9/11/01
Subject:

I think I am the only person left in this building. I don't know what to say or do. But as bad as everything looks, I think it's going to get much, much, worse.

Ryan

* * *

From: Michelle
To: Josh
Sent: 9/11/01
Subject: Are you Ok?

Josh,

How are you? I hope you are okay.

Michelle

* * *

As "cold" as the advertising business is supposed to be, I don't see or feel coldness often, if at all. Maybe I'm lucky, or maybe it's what I put out there is what I get back in return, but I find the people I work with, as well as my clients, pleasant for the most part. Michelle's simple email sticks out to me as one of pure concern.

I know I have been instructed by parents, doctors, health-classes, and even television commercials to use protection in order to protect myself from catching STDs. I once learned to wear a seatbelt to protect myself in the event of a car accident, and police try their best to enforce their use. Alarmingly, however, no one has ever advised me, at any point in my life, to protect my mental self. So much emphasis gets placed on the physical, yet the mental gets slighted. For a field labeled as cut-throat, I would think it would be…cut-throat. But it isn't, at least not for me.

There's a saying when life gives lemons, turn them into lemonade. I like to think about what happens before life bequeaths those lemons. To get those lemons, I need to plant the seeds for a lemon tree. So, if I plant those seeds, I will reap what I sow. Hence, what I put out there is what I will get back in return. I apply the lemon notion to everyday life, in that I put out what I want back in return. And there is nothing wrong with wanting lemons, I can make quite delicious lemonade once I have them, I can even make pink lemonade (just add strawberries) but the key is I know what I want and plant the seeds for what I want. When I want positive, healthy relationships with my clients, I project a positive and healthy energy in order that I can receive the same in return.

* * *

From: Michelle
To: All
Sent: 9/13/01
Subject: Unite Against Terrorism

This message was forwarded to me. The originator is unknown to me, but the message
is important. Please pass it on. Michelle

This Friday Night at 7:00 p.m. get outside. If you are in a car, then pull over and get out, and if you are inside your house, get yourself outside. Wherever you happen to be on Friday at 7, get yourself outside and light a candle. As a country, we have to remain united and do this together. We need to let the entire world know we are still one and terrorism will not be tolerated. We are strong and can and will remain united. Be sure to forward the contents of this message to as many people as you can, and encourage them to do the same. Everyone across the United States needs to be a part of this. So please take a moment to forward it now, and please participate on Friday night at 7:00 p.m. to give the message to the world that The United States will not now, and will never tolerate terrorism.

Thank you so much.
The world will see our glorious message of peace and unity.
Michelle

* * *

Charlie Casso

My mom and I step onto our porch and light a candle on Friday the 14th at 7:00. Most of the porches on our block in Bensonhurst, Brooklyn have combinations of family members on them. Little kids tug at their parents' clothing on one porch. On another, a husband and wife hold a candle between them. The experience, seeing so many people unite for a cause, makes me choke back tears. I had not received this email when it was sent because the email server at work was down, but word has spread so much so that my mom and I still manage to participate. After the community spreads its message of peace and tranquility, I venture into the city with John and Steven to see "The Glass House" at the unusually quiet AMC Lincoln Center in order to send a personal message on behalf of NYC and me. I, no, we, will not be held down.

* * *

From: Randy
To: Josh
Sent: 9/17/01
Subject: Is everyone well?

Josh, it has been impossible to get through to your office via telephone. Additionally, your website is down. I'm aware of how close your offices are to the WTC and this worries me. Is everyone well? Please, when you can, if you can, contact me.

Thank you,
Randy

* * *

The location of my office is a little close to the WTC. Actually, it's a lot close. I spend many a lunch hour at the WTC. Either I visit the WTC or go to the South Street Seaport. Right before 9/11, no more than a week before it, I visit the Warner Brothers Store inside the World Trade Center to purchase a gift for my niece. While in the store, I see a Gossamer plush doll I want for myself. I pick it up in my hands, and feel its fine, orange hair with my fingertips. I do not purchase the doll, even though Gossamer has always been a favorite character of mine. I laugh uncontrollably when I watch Bugs Bunny give Gossamer a manicure. Part of the reason I don't get the Gossamer plush doll is because I think buying one for myself is a little, just a little, childish. My inner child always wants to play, but at the time I say, well, I can think about it, I don't have to get it today. The doll I hold in my hands and leave there, well, I can't help but think it got burnt, charred, and disintegrated. Sometimes when my inner child wants to play, I have to give in. The ability to play may not be there tomorrow. The child inside me cries when he thinks about what must pass before the doll's eyes on the morning of September 11th.

* * *

From: Josh
To: Randy
Sent: 9/17/01
Subject: Re: Is everyone well?

Hi Randy,

Thank you for your concern, as far as I know we are all okay. I'm writing you this message from home. Wednesday (9/19) will be the first day that the whole company will be back in the office. I will be sure to contact you then with an update.

Thanks again,
Josh
Regional Sales Assistant
212-XXX-XXXX

* * *

From: Randy
To: Josh
Sent: 9/17/01
Subject: Re: Is everyone well?

Josh,

I'm so glad to hear that you are ok. It's one thing to watch what is happening on the news, but it's another thing completely to know that someone I talk to and deal with is so close. I was quite worried, so thank you for the response.

How about we use the same ad that is being placed in the September issue for the October issue as well? I know we wanted to run a new ad, with new copy, but I think that's going to be difficult now. We can try for that for the November issue. There are more important issues to deal with, so a new ad can wait.

By the way, I didn't receive a copy of the September issue, which is odd.

Randy

* * *

From: Josh
To: Randy
Sent: 9/17/01
Subject: Re: Is everyone well?

Randy,

Sounds like a plan. I had not received a copy of the September issue myself before everything happened on the 11th. They must be on their way, I can't imagine them running late. If I have copies when I get back to the office I'll send some your way :0)

Keep in touch and thanks again,

Josh Conti
Regional Sales Assistant
212-XXX-XXXX

* * *

From: Randy
To: Josh
Sent: 9/17/01
Subject: Re: Is everyone well?

Josh,

Glad to hear it. I checked into the new ad, and we can definitely have something ready in time for the November issue. I'm thinking that the copy date will be around October 15th or so.
Thanks again Josh,

Randy

* * *

I include a smiley face in my email to Randy in which we discuss ad placement. I can't help it. I can be professional but I simply refuse to forget there is an "I" in professional, which reminds me to be myself. Without the "I," the word becomes "professonal," which sounds as if I'm about to profess something to someone and, frankly, that's not the case. While I admire people who can be stern professionals and not inject their personality into their work, I admire myself enough to be comfortable with who I am and to let others see me for that very same person, smiley face and all.

Doing business with advertisers becomes tough, but some continue to show support, at least initially, by not pulling their ads. A client who lets ads run shows a phenomenal level of support. The advertisers show faith all will be fine. I completely understand, from the advertisers' perspectives, why they would not want their ads to run in issues that come out soon after 9/11. When a magazine or newspaper includes an article on 9/11, the companies and products near that article become associated with the tragedy. That is by far the worst connection a consumer can make with a product. Additionally, the events will undoubtedly have a negative effect on the economy.

The combination of the aforementioned reasons makes incentive wane for advertisers to continue their ad placement. Not only does Randy allow his advertisement to run, but he also decides to have us run a pickup. A pickup, a repeat of an ad we ran previously, means we don't have to worry about the receipt of new materials in the mail. Item inspection and postal precautions have increased significantly, resulting in delays receiving items sent through the post office. Randy's choice to run a repeat of an ad that has already run with us lets me exhale a sigh of relief.

Not oddly enough, unfortunately, I experience
someone taking advantage of the post office
problems after 9/11. I order an autographed
photograph of Nicole Kidman and Ewan McGregor
from "Moulin Rouge" which has become one of my
favorite movies of all time and came out on June 1,
2001, right at the start of Summer of Love Redux, as
I refer to it.

I had been looking forward to "Moulin Rouge"
for about six months. "Moulin Rouge" was a pretty
high profile movie which came out on the heels of
the Nicole Kidman / Tom Cruise divorce. Most of
the time I was looking forward to the movie, I was
attached to Drug-addled Ex. So of course when the
movie hit the theaters he thought of me. I couldn't
help but think of the comparison between Nicole
and myself. She left someone after being with him a
for long time and being held down by him, not
letting her star completely shine because of him, not
being fully happy because of him. And now she is
free, and I am too. In her emancipation she sings,
she dances, and she makes millions. Well, two out
three for me aren't so bad. Over the course of the
summer, I see the movie six times and I think that
will be it. But then I meet Drug-addled Ex's friend
Wilson one night while out at a club in Brooklyn
called Spectrum.

As a Deborah Cox remix beats through the club,
Wilson approaches me, very straight forwardly, and
tells me, not asks me, "You're Josh."

My left eyebrow shoots up as I question, "How do you know me?"

He reveals, "I'm Wilson. I'm a friend of [Drug-addled Ex.]"

"You and I never met before."

"I know. I have seen you in photographs at his place."

I think, "Slut!" automatically. First of all, Drug-addled Ex has never had a friend "Wilson" I knew of. Secondly, Drug-addled Ex sleeps with all of his friends at one point or another. Not a single person exists who he has been friends with whom he has not slept with. I'm not being judgmental, but what a slut.

The gay community, at large, is one in which, not atypically, a guy sleeps with, at one point or another, or several points, his friends. I don't get this. I never sleep with friends, and I can't imagine why a person would. If a guy finds himself attracted to someone, then he should get the chutzpah (if Jewish), cajones (Catholic / Italian), or balls (plain American), and go for it. The "it" could be a date, a relationship, or a one-night-stand, but those are pretty much all of the "its." So many people exist out there and I just can't imagine why a guy would want to fool around with someone who he wants in his life for the long haul.

Already out of the relationship with Drug-addled Ex for months now, I am compelled to ask Wilson, "Why does he still have pictures of me out in his apartment?"

"Valid question," Wilson admits. "I'd want to know the same thing myself if I were you. He doesn't have the pictures out in frames or anything, but he talks about you a lot. He asked me to keep an eye out for you while I'm out and about. That's why he showed me the pictures."

"Keep an eye out for me? Why?"

"He wants to know if you are seeing anyone, stuff like that."

So, he wants Wilson to spy on me and report back to him with any news regarding lovers or, not to sound too Jane Erye-ish, or Jane Eerie, dalliances. I can't believe it, but I kind of can believe it.

Naturally, I ask Wilson, "And how long this has been going on?"

"Just about a month."

"Have you told him anything?" I inquire.

"Well, I have seen you before tonight."

"What does that mean?"

"I told him about you and that guy against the fence."

Confused, I respond, "What?"

"You know what I'm talking about, you were all over each other. The big guy. Against the fence across the street."

It clicks. During a moment of weakness, in my defense, I did make out with someone against the fence across the street from Spectrum.

"Who was he?" asks Wilson.

"Not that it's your business, but that was my first ex, John, if you must know. And how dare you report back to [Drug-addled Ex]."

"I'm not asking for him," responds Wilson, "I'm asking because I want to know. Yes, he showed me pictures of you so I'd know who you were, and yes I was supposed to, and did, report back to him, but I would like to get to know you myself."

He Julius Ceasar-ed Drug-addled Ex! A man who goes for what he wants, I have to respect that.

Wilson asks, "Would you like to do something one day, go on a date?"

I need to avenge Drug-addled Ex for having enlisted a lover-cum-spy-cum-Brutus/traitor to aid him. So, after listening to Wilson with both ears and plotting with what lie between them, I realize I can definitely go see *Moulin Rouge* again. If I go to see it with Wilson, chances are he will mention he saw the movie to Drug-addled Ex, and then he, in-turn, will think of me and possibly put two and two together. Wilson is a former marine, so going to see *Moulin Rouge* would not be his first choice. (For that matter it probably wouldn't even be his tenth choice.)

"Sure. Have you seen *Moulin Rouge*?"

"No. What is that?"

"It's a movie, I've been wanting to see it again."

"Sounds good to me then. Are you up for hanging out tonight?"

Hanging out tonight is gay code for get biblical — if, in some new version of the Bible, gays abound and they abound on each other.

"Not tonight, Wilson. If it were earlier it might be a different story," I reply. Going home with Wilson tonight would be like having him buy the cow later when he drank the milk for free tonight.

At about two-thirty in the morning I would typically take a cab home, but I figure why not have Wilson, the former marine and presumably current bouncy bouncy partner of Drug-addled Ex, walk me home. I may play blonde, but I am not blonde. No way will Wilson walk me all the way home. No, there will be no all the way tonight. Instead, he will walk me just close enough but yet seemingly so far away. We walk most of the way home and stop walking when we get a mere three blocks away.

I mention my concern for him, that all the while we walked he needed to go in the opposite direction. He figures he'll walk me all the way home, ever the gentleman. Don't be silly though, I can make it on my own, I'm a big boy. Conveniently, but not accidentally, we happen to stand in front of the twenty-four hour car service on 18th avenue. I press him to get a cab home and not to worry about me. Also, I remind him about *Moulin Rouge*. After all, I can't leave him feeling that blue.

Wilson and I see *Moulin Rouge* on the evening of August 26th, at the AMC theater on 42nd street in Times Square. This marks the last time I see Wilson, for two reasons. Primarily, I only want to see the movie with him because, although I want to see it again, I also want to have it get back to Drug-addled Ex. A final act of passive aggressiveness. I may be passive aggressive, but at least I own it. The second reason for not seeing Wilson again is plainly and simply because the night of the movie is the same night I go on to meet, and become enamored with, Steven.

While taking advantage of people isn't nice, it happens. The autographed photograph I ordered of Nicole and Ewan from *Moulin Rouge* doesn't arrive, the seller blames it on the post office, and I do not receive a refund. People can be so cruel.

* * *

From: John
To: Josh
Sent: 9/17/01
Subject: Hi

Hey Josh,

I am not sure if you are at work yet. Your office, I think, may still be closed.
So if I don't hear back from you I'm going to assume it's still closed. Are you feeling okay?

Did you manage to do anything this weekend?
Able to get your mind off what happened? I
really hope you're doing all right. I realize it is
a completely different experience from your
shoes than mine. I have a friend who lives by
Union Square and she is not handling what
happened well at all. She seems, well,
traumatized by everything that happened. It
makes me worry about you because you were
right there.

Josh, if you want to talk about
anything, I'll be at work for a while, so
feel free to call me. You can also email
if you would rather.

Talk to you soon.
John

* * *

John does not receive an email response from me this morning. After I speak with Randy through email, simply because his email is the most recent of the inordinate amount of emails in my mailbox, I turn off my home computer and lie in bed. I can't return to work yet. The offices remain closed due to their proximity to the WTC and people are not allowed into the immediate area. John, however, happens to be the very first person to reach me on my cell phone on the morning of the 11th. He's the perfect person to speak with in a time in need. John provides a sympathetic shoulder to cry on and focuses on my pain and needs instead of his own.

The first reason I ever opened my mouth had to be to complain. As a baby, I want food so I open my mouth and let out a wail. A dirty diaper necessitates a need to be changed, so I open my mouth and cry aloud. I'm gassy, so I open my mouth and… eventually the wailing turns into speech. I form words, form sentences, form clearer ways to communicate precisely what I want to complain or wail about. If survival of the fittest imparts anything, it teaches there is an innate quality of competitiveness alive in the living world. Competitiveness creates rivalry between people in a fete a fete wherein a person who accomplishes "A" meets with another person who accomplishes "A" and "B" and vocalizes his or her accomplishment. As I work so close to the WTC, and literally run for my life on 9/11, I find solace in John's email wherein he does not try to outdo my story with his own or that of another person he knows. John's simple sentence, "I know it is a completely different experience from your shoes than mine," is a rare gem I find where he simply acknowledges my plight and, even though he may be suffering from a similar plight, puts aside his innate desire in order to help me.

Since the offices remain closed, I have more than an ample amount of me-time. I have difficulty sleeping at night. The process of falling asleep becomes especially daunting, as I fear the onset of sleep because with sleep comes the nightmares. I shudder at the thought of the nightmares that jolt me back to an even more frightening reality. I lie down and watch television on my side, I pull the comforter up over me, and I pray the comforter provides the comfort its name so sweetly proffers.

I lie down, wait for sleep to come, fear that sleep will come, and find little solace in the programming on late night television. And then a moment of divine intervention happens. A glimmer of hope flashes across the television screen. The sight entrances me so immeasurably I practically feel my eyes dilate as they take in the spectacle and grandeur.

Britney Spears, wearing an Elvis Presley outfit, flashes across the screen one more time. The commercial on HBO advertises a Britney Spears Live from Las Vegas concert on November 18th at the MGM Grand in Las Vegas. Could this be the beacon of light that will guide me back to myself, and help me to escape the dreariness of the events that recently transpired? If Britney can go back in time and echo the best of a better time, a time before September 11th, then I will surely be able to do the same. All it takes is a Britney commercial to restore the mirror-adorned-glitter-ball that is a gay man's heart. I will get myself to Las Vegas again, and get myself to that concert. But first, I must get back to work.

* * *

Charlie Casso

From: Ryan
To: (Synergy sales team)
Sent: 9/18/01
Subject: SENDING ADS TO SYNERGY

As one of the innumerable consequences of the tragedy in New York City, ad materials sent through the mail either may never be received at all or may be received so late that they won't be able to be included in the appropriate issue(s) anyhow. This also goes for ad materials that advertisers are currently submitting. These packages may never arrive here, or arrive horrifically late.

As a result, please instruct your clients, specifically those who are used to sending film, or other hard copy materials, to convert their materials to an electronic format. Submitting the ad materials electronically, at least for the time being, will be the only way to prevent ad materials from being lost or arriving late. Under normal circumstances, clients would send their materials to an ftp site however this site is currently not functioning. Please have clients submit the pages via ftp directly to the printer.

If a client refuses to send anything other than film, please have them send the hard copy materials for all magazines to the following address via overnight service: (Address deleted).

Thanks,
Ryan

* * *

The submission of ad materials, typically the easiest part of the advertising process, now requires extra care and new protocols due to postal scrutiny in a post 9/11 world. Concerns about the submission of advertising materials appear to be just the tip of the iceberg. Many of my clients send hard copy materials. The best way to ensure the ads run as intended is to send in hard copy materials. Electronic submissions leave the magazines open to receiving complaints that the ads don't run as intended because the color seems off or another technical detail is amiss.

* * *

From: Cecile
To: All
Sent: 9/18/01
Subject: Employee Information / Helpdesk

Synergy has set up, for the time being, a private employee information website.

You may log on to the site at http://(address deleted). The username is synergy and your password is your last name. Please be sure to use all lower case letters, as it is case sensitive. For those who need access to the helpdesk, please use the new helpdesk phone number. Please use 212-XXX-XXXX for all helpdesk issues. E-mailing issues or concerns to the attention of the helpdesk at help@XXXX.com, is always preferred, even if you also use the phone line.

Thank you for your attention to these changes. If you have any questions regarding these changes, please let me know.

Thank you,
Cecile
Director of Human Resources

* * *

From: Shannon
To: All
Sent: 9/18/01
Subject: UPDATE-NYC-
SYNERGY

Due to the location of the Synergy offices and the recent, horrific occurrences at the World Trade Center, our offices are closed, and will remain closed though September 18th.
We expect the offices to re-open on the morning of the 19th. Please contact me as soon as possible regarding your inclusion in upcoming features of Synergy such as our Synergy Standouts, Synergy Showcase, and Synergy Standards. In your email, please include the specs regarding ad size, preferred placement, selected section, etc.

Although the offices are closed I will do my best to answer any questions or concerns you may have. So if you have any, please do not hesitate to contact me. Your ads remain a priority.

Postal issues will undoubtedly be a concern, so if you already mailed materials, please send them electronically. Include information as follows:

Company name, Contact name, Billing
address, and Ad size/Package.
Materials: whether pickup or email.
Price as quoted or as appears on listing form.
Should any questions or concerns arise, please do not
hesitate to contact me.

Thank you,
Shannon

* * *

Stoic. Shannon keeps her eye on the prize. I
guess that's what made her such a valuable
companion to trek across the bridge with. She has a
goal and goes for it. Shannon sends this email the
day before the offices re-open. Even though I don't
know how it will be possible, I think things will go
right back to normal.

Chapter Eight: Welcome Back to Work, Now Try to Breathe

From: Cecile
To: All
Sent: 9/19/01
Subject: Moment of Silence/1PM today

Let's come together not only as an office or as a company, but as part of a nation united. Today, at 1:00 p.m. Eastern, let's take two minutes out of our busy day to devote to those we have lost, that which we have gone through, everything we pray for, and for ourselves.

For those of us located in the New York office, let's meet in the conference room on the twenty-second floor.

September 11, 2001 has touched us all, and we all need to come together to acknowledge that and show solidarity in the face of this adversity.

This moment of silence is extended not just to the New York office, but also to the offices located in Europe and Asia, as well as all of our other offices, as you are undoubtedly affected as well.

Thank you,
Cecile

* * *

A moment of silence, mere blocks away from the WTC, requires strength on the part of all those who participate, as this is where it all went down. No one cries during the moment of silence in the conference room. Everyone, in their business gear, stares at the grey carpeted floor in front of them. A couple of eyes take quick glances at the others occasionally, but then quickly resume their focus on the floor. We remain shocked by the recent events, kind of like fish when the water is changed in their bowl: the fish remain in the same location but something has changed and that change affects those involved. Even when I try to put 9/11 out of my mind I can't succeed because a thick, choking, burning smell pervades the air, every minute of every day. Additionally, I have apocalyptical amounts of work to accomplish and the pressure placed upon me becomes monumental. The combination of what I have gone through, having this inordinate amount of work to handle, and having to do the work in the midst of the scene where the towers collapsed amounts to a test of endurance, stamina, and mental wellness.

* * *

From: Lance
To: All
Sent: 9/19/01
Subject: Click to Help

Hey there everyone,

If we can all take a second or two to have an impact we can truly do wonders for this country. All you have to do is visit the following website and simply click where it says "Help Us Help Others." That's all. Seriously, all you have to do is click that button that says "Help Us Help Others." When you click, a corporate sponsor donates to one of the many groups involved in the recovery efforts in NYC and D.C. I promise you that your contribution does not cost you a thing, other than the second or two spent visiting the site and clicking the button. I believe there's a cap, so you can only visit and click once a day, but every little bit helps, so please I cannot encourage you enough. Additionally, please feel free to forward this information to everyone in your address book.
Together we can make a world of difference.

http://www.helpXXXX.com
Best Regards,
Lance
Southwest District Manager

* * *

From: Cecile
To: All
Sent: 9/19/01
Subject: Re: Click to Help

Good Day All,

   Remember before you visit internet sites, or consider giving personal information to anyone in an effort to help, that there are going to be quite a number of people out there taking advantage of the kindness of others. We all have hearts and we all want to help, but some people are going to be duped by others with less than noble motives. As if this tragedy that has just happened isn't bad enough, please also be aware that you need to be cognizant of what websites you visit and what ways are the best to help. I am not certain regarding the legitimacy of the help that the website Lance forwarded, but I want to make sure that you evaluate for yourself, as best as you can, the legitimacy of any causes that seek your help. One thing you should be aware of is the fact that businesses and corporations will contribute directly to causes. They will not, however, go through another avenue altogether, such as this website link that was forwarded. On that note, I stress again, please proceed with caution before becoming involved in help efforts.
   Please do not misinterpret what I am saying. Get involved, help, just do so with eyes wide open. This is a great time to help people, yes, but it also a great opportunity for others to take advantage of those who want to help. Do not fall prey to them. Do not lie on your back and let these people take what they want from you. Be aware. Remember, you can say no.

Many legitimate organizations exist which do not solicit contributions. The American Red Cross comes to mind as one such organization. You can donate to the ARC, but they will never, ever ask for or solicit contributions from people. These types of organizations remain the best ones to contribute to as they have good reputations, are reliable, and will benefit a wealth of people and do a wealth of good.

Should you have concerns about an organization, the ARC or another, I invite you to contact me. I just don't want to see anyone trying to help, during this time of tragedy, get taken advantage of and get hurt.

Thank you,
Cecile
Director of Human Resources

* * *

For every tragedy that occurs, someone will try to take advantage of it in order to gain something for him or herself. Unfortunate, but true. I can't ascertain the legitimacy of the forward Lance sent, but, regardless, thieves in the proverbial temple are never welcomed.

Regarding thieves in the temple, I visit Union Square with Steven several times immediately after September 11th. Union Square marks the closest the public can get to the downtown area. As such, people who either want to pay tribute to or grieve for those who were lost on the infamous day visit the park at Union Square and adorn the area with flowers of every kind and color. Amidst the throngs of people, flowers, and candles, are stands set up with vendors who hawk 9/11 themed shirts, hats, buttons, pins, and other accoutrements. The first thought that pops into my mind when I notice the people who sell their wares is of Jesus overturning the tables. I become so angry when I see what's happening I completely understand why he had overturned those tables. These people exhibit a lack of scruples, plain and simple. How dare they try to capitalize off of the suffering of others by selling such grave memorabilia?

"Steven," I ask, "what do you think of all these buttons and whatnot?"

"It's New York."

"Yeah, but, don't you think it's sad?"

"How so?"

"Maybe disrespectful is the better word. Don't you think it's a bit harsh to have buttons and shirts with 9/11 printed on them, and to be selling them here while people are grieving?"

"It's the way of the world. If there wasn't a market for it then they wouldn't be here."

"It's too early for this. People look for their brothers, sisters, mothers, fathers, whoever, they look for the missing and they see this," I point at the table next to me as I feel something in me rise. It must be conviction. With conviction I continue, "They shouldn't have to see this. It's just not right. It's not the time to…" puke. What rises isn't conviction. It's my lunch. For the fourth time in my life, I puke. Mom always says real Italians don't throw up, and I very rarely do. The vendors at Union Square strike such a nerve in me that I cannot contain myself, or my lunch.

"What the hell you do?" the vendor next to me bellows in broken English.

"Oh my God, I'm so…" and it happens again. More puke, and on the vendor's table no less.

I want to dig a hole in the park and bury myself to escape humiliation, however that would take too long. So what can I do? I run.

As a native New Yorker, even I would think I would see the vendors with their wares and just shrug it off. After all, it's New York, where I can't take a simple subway ride without being approached at least once or twice by strangers who ask me for the same thing: money. When panhandlers walk through the subway cars and plead their cases, mostly without convincing stories, or worse, while wearing nice sneakers, I have to admit I turn a blind eye. There's a method to my seeming apathy. I've seen people of all ages plead for money on the train. Some have even been as young as five or six years old. I watch as this occurs and I think, gee, if I made about ten dollars in two minutes, I probably wouldn't ever be inspired to work either. I could make a career as a panhandler. A youth, a six year old who asks for money, merely with an outstretched hand or in exchange for a quick impromptu dance on a moving train, attempts to inspire empathy. My, they are so young, my, that is such a shame. The shame is the children receive positive reinforcement for doing exactly what they are not supposed to be doing. They use their government issued subway passes, which should be getting them to school and home, in order to panhandle for money while they shirk their educational responsibilities. When I turn a blind eye, I hope these children find a better way to make a living, perhaps by going to school and making something of themselves.

Hence, I welcome Cecile's response regarding solicitation. People of all ages, races, nationalities, and any conceivable modifying descriptors, need guidance regarding how to help others. Thankfully, many people are naturally inclined to help others in whatever manner they can, but sometimes instead of helping, they further hinder the actual growth of the other.

From: Josh
To: Steven
Sent: 9/19/01
Subject:

Oh yeah, good to be back at work. The lights keep
going out. The first time was especially nice because a

couple of the women screamed. Oh yeah, good to be back. (Sarcasm deeply intended.)

See you this evening :0)
Josh

* * *

From: Steven
To: Josh
Sent: 9/19/01
Subject: RE:

I see that you're not having the greatest day back at work. Sorry. And, ummm, I unfortunately have to say the same. Guess where I was. I was just outside. Not for a stroll, or for a snack, no, no.

Everyone in my office just had to evacuate the premicis- er premises (hard to spell) because of a bomb threat.

Can't wait to see you and escape from here,
Steven

* * *

Charlie Casso

When I get off the train in the downtown area, by my office and the WTC, I come face to face with a bevy of armed guards. The guards wear full camouflage fatigues, helmets, and boots. More accurately, it appears as if G.I. Joe and all of his friends have infiltrated my work environs. While this would normally seem like fantasy-land to a gay man in his early twenties, the reality is anything but that.

A myriad of changes are now imposed upon the downtown area. I must show my work identification in order to walk down the streets. The streets themselves have a muddy grey color, and every window has a thick coat of soot and ash. The air itself has a muddy yellow haze. Stores, sidewalks, cars, windows, and street-signs have a dingy-yellowish tint. It must be all of the debris and particles that remain in the air. Occasionally, a message such as "God Bless America" can be found, such as the one drawn in the dust on the Hallmark store's window. The workday in the downtown area always starts off with a sense of uneasiness, especially since the wreckage from September 11th remains visible in the background. Behind the army men, the remnants of structures seem to weep as pieces of damaged buildings hang downward.

Charlie Casso

Once at work, bomb scares and lights that go out all day just make it all the worse. The smell of death in the air interrupts attempts at typing up proposals, putting presentations together, and talking with clients. The stench burns my throat and makes me feel dry and thirsty. My esophagus feels chafed raw, about to bleed. Then, while I try my best to focus on the work in front of me, all of the lights go off. Blackness envelops me and I suddenly find myself left in complete and utter darkness, knowing only a few days ago terrorists flew planes into the skyscrapers that were once next door. As oppressive and exhausting as the days become, I try my hardest not to let the days get me down. I still go out with my boyfriend (and Steven too). My boyfriend, of course, being New York City. No terrorists will ever tear us asunder.

Chapter Nine: Trying to Reclaim Old New York and My Old Life

On September 19th, Steven and I meet up with each other in front of the Virgin Megastore at Union Square after work. The Virgin Megastore serves as our usual meeting place, because it's equidistant between our offices. When we go in to browse around, we find Fiona Apple doing an autograph signing to promote her newest cd. We look from afar. After high school I was a pretty big Fiona Apple fan, but over the years my affinity for her has waned a bit.

* * *

From: Steven
To: Josh
Sent: 9/20/01
Subject: Fiona

Josh,

Seeing as how I had the pleasure of being in your midst yesterday while this all went down, I had to document our experience, since I know you'll want to remember it forever. (I think a lot of people share these same feelings to be completely truthful.) Anyway, I hope it helps make your day even a little bit better. If it does, then I've done my job. Can't wait to talk to you tonight…

SAMOOCHES!!…Steven

Brace yourself. I saw her. She basically appeared in a bubble that descended to Earth, well, specifically, Union Square. I didn't actually see this firsthand or anything, but I have to imagine that that is how she alighted upon the penultimate shopping place in the universe, the Virgin Megastore. I originally went there to spend some time and catch up with Josh, and then this happened. We were in the Megastore and, well, she appeared. The one and only Fiona Divinity Apple. The air was electrifying. Her scent was intoxicating. It smelled like Bob Ross, Jimi Hendrix, and Leonardo DaVinci rolled into one. It was the smell of unrestrained, pure artistry. Someone needs to bottle it and sell it, because I guarantee world peace in less than seven seconds of inhaling that scent. Goddess / creator that she is. It all made sense, because what other entity could change the atmosphere so, but Fiona Apple?

I heard someone scream out, "Hey, where's your swan dress?" This was followed by the iciest chill in the air I have ever experienced. I caught a glance of Fiona, and I have to admit I didn't know her eyes were so startlingly red. Children screamed in their carriages. Someone else asked above the crowd, "Are you really going to do that reality show I heard about?" At this, the whole of the pop music section rumbled. I watched as Britney and Christina CDs fell to the ground and cracked open. In a snarl befitting the demons of hell, Fiona bellowed, "I'm an artist. Arrrrrt-isssssst!" (As she said this, her tongue snaked out and flickered.) She continued, "Reality is for the masses. I am not." As the gigantic NSYNC poster burst into flames overhead, parents and children, young and old, scrambled. What appeared to be a wormhole to another dimension opened up right smack dab in the middle of the Virgin Megastore. Fiona leapt in with one last monstrous glare at the remains of the crowd. Those who hadn't fled, I mean we have lived through much worse after all, remained and filled their baskets with Virgin goodies.

The ten-year old next to me looked at her basket with a disapproving scowl. She picked up her Mandy Moore CD, handed it her mom, and said, "Mommy she's mean. I don't want it anymore."

* * *

Steven's wit and inventiveness amuse me. His quirkiness serves as a plus too. While in the Union Square area, I see the park overflows with contributions from those who grieve and make an effort for others to have a place to grieve, and to hope, as well. Printouts which feature photographs of loved ones who have been missing since 9/11 adorn the gates and fences in the park as family members seek information about the ones they love. The piece that sticks with me the most is the John Wayne cutout next to the arrangement of flowers in the shape of the U.S. flag.

I wonder who has written, "This is no time for cowboys"? Did the person who left the John Wayne cutout do the writing? Did someone else see the display and decide to comment on it? The juxtaposition of images, flowers, and text in this scene captures just a snippet of what occurs, not just in the minds of New Yorkers, but in most people's minds. Well, okay, mine. All of these different, at times conflicting, and at times complimenting ideas and thoughts combine together in a cacophony not of sound, but of thought.

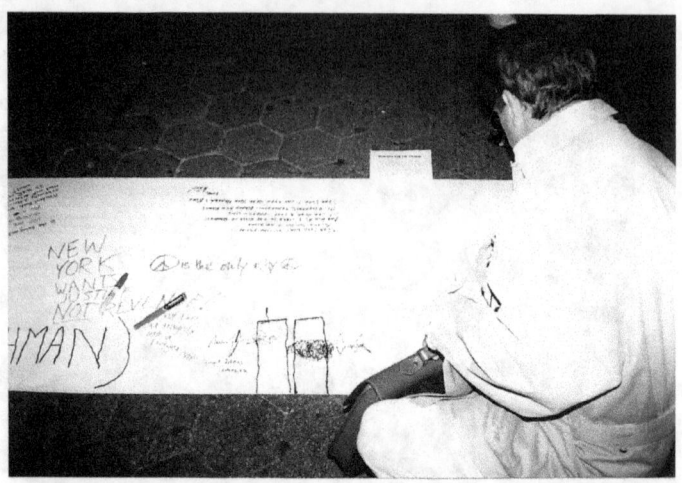

From: Josh
To: Phoebe
Sent: 9/20/01
Subject:

Okay, so I have to take off two days next week. The Monday and the Tuesday I guess? Arrgh, and I don't have anything planned. As for the New Orleans trip, I still have to book a hotel. Double arrgh.

At least, as I said, Glitter starts tomorrow, and it's going to be playing at both the AMC theatre and the Chelsea theatre. (The latter of which I think would be the more festive one, since most of my people love Mariah.) Anyway, oy vey. So much stuff to ponder. Do you have any days you need to take off by Sept 30?

Josh

* * *

From: Phoebe
To: Josh
Sent: 9/20/01
Subject: Re:

Oh, Josh, let's get things worked out. Let me first say that you're so lucky you get to take days off. That's not an option for me, unfortunately. They'd sooner fire me… wait, let me think. Actually, it doesn't matter if I were to take days off, I'm sure they want to fire me regardless. Can they bring stoning back? You know, line up all the managers, give them each a little mound of rocks and stones by their feet. Someone, maybe Cecile, can start the countdown. Three, two, one, and then aiyeeeee!!!!! I hope stoning doesn't come back in vogue, because I really think they want me out like a rotten molar. To be on the safe side, if one even exists, I know I shouldn't take any days off.

You however, you're a different story. They're pleased as punch, and I use that term kind of loosely because I don't really know where it comes from exactly, but they are pleased as punch that you're here. So I'm sure that they'll accommodate whatever you want, without question. It's easier though to take off two days in a row.

Whatever you decide, I'd just try not to be here on a Friday, because that'd bite the big one. At least get the weekend off to a great start by using one of the days there. I'd suggest either bookending M/F so you only work mid-week or T/W or W/TH, so you have the week broken up nicely.

Regardless, you're lucky enough to have John to hang around with. You'll definitely have a good time. And on the off chance that you get bored you can do some research on that stoning thing. I might need to get informed A.S.A.P.!

Can you tell me how to carry over my unused days? I don't know what I need to do to carry them over but I obviously can't take them now, and I don't want to lose them either.

Get your butt moving regarding the hotel for your stay in New Orleans. Those prices will skyrocket if you don't get it booked soon.

Let me know about the days and don't forget to book the hotel!

* * *

Work mandates I visit New Orleans. I need to attend a trade convention there and I seriously want to extend my stay for a couple of additional days since I've always wanted to go to NOLA. New Orleans, the home to voodoo, Anne Rice, the French Quarter, and Mardi Gras, allures me. Phoebe serves as a stellar source for advice about NOLA, since she used to live there. So I pick her brain for a bit, hoping to get the inside scoop on the Big Easy, which, for once, does not refer to my salacious friend John. While on a run across the street for some morning carbs, I ask Phoebe, "So, you lived In New Orleans, where should I stay while I'm there?"

"You have to stay in the French Quarter while you are there. Other areas are pretty, don't get me wrong, but a block in the wrong direction here or there and it's a world of hurt just waiting for you. There are some scary areas."

"Oh," I utter, "well, all right, stay in the French Quarter. Got it. Where though, like any hotels or bed and breakfasts you'd recommend?"

"Well, see, I didn't really stay at hotels or B and Bs. I squatted."

"Squatted?"

"Squatted."

"I heard you clearly, I'm just... what do you mean you squatted?"

"Oh, my little Josh, so naive. Squatters are people who sit around the park, or on the street, and well, squat. They stay there. It's pretty much where they live. I only did it because I didn't have a place to stay. The streets were mostly clean so I figured why not. I'd be outside with a cup in front of me, listening to people play live jazz music in front of the park at Jackson Square, and by the end of the day I'd have a cup full of money to go drinking with at night."

"Listen, free spirit, I'm not squatting."

"So check the places in the French Quarter and show me which ones you like. I'll tell you which streets are better. That should help. You'll have fun regardless, it's still New Orleans, the Big Easy."

"Why is it called the Big Easy anyhow?" I ask.

"I'm not sure. Everyone really is easy there though. So be careful. You don't want to come home with crabs."

"Phoebe," I say, shaking my head, "you know I don't do fish."

* * *

From: Josh
To: Steven
Sent: 9/20/01
Subject:

Morning Handsome,

So, I have to take off two days by Sept 30. They are not going to allow us to carry them over despite what happened last week. I'm going to be away Oct 2-4, so I don't want to take off the end of next week since that will be rather close to the business trip. That leaves me with Monday and Tuesday to take off, yet I have no plans to do anything great since it was unanticipated.

I decided I am not going to try to alter my New Orleans trip as I have been looking forward to it for so long. I just have to book the hotel for my personal nights there and then all will be totally set. Phoebe is going to help me find a great place since she knows NOLA well. I think everything is in order now, it's just that I have to find something cool to do on Monday and Tuesday.

All of that decision making, and its not even 10 o'clock yet.

Josh

* * *

From: Josh
To: John
Sent: 9/21/01
Subject: Hey!

Hey John,

Can I twist your arm and convince you to see Glitter tonight? I'm sure you're rolling your eyes as you read this, but you have to admit it would be entertaining. You'll finally be able to meet Steven too. Phoebe won't get out of seeing Glitter tonight either, so we could all catch up. Hopefully you'll come?

Till later,
Josh

* * *

From: John
To: Josh
Sent: 9/21/01
Subject: Re: Hey!

Hey Josh,

Aww, thank you for inviting me to go to see Glitter with you guys. I am sure the movie would be fun. Unfortunately, I have to go to my boyfriend's to visit his family. His grandmother is in the hospital, she is having more than her fair share of problems. She's on dialysis and that really takes it out of a person, or so I hear. He's rightfully upset about it and her wants to visit his family. As alluring as Glitter would be, I have to go with him. Thank you again though.

I'm really glad I just received your invite though, because I forgot to email you earlier. A really good opportunity was forwarded to me and I think you would be interested for sure. I'm pasting it below, so be sure to read it. I really think you'll like it. The friend who forwarded it to me told me to invite as many people as my heart desired, and so, well, read on and enjoy. And don't forget you can go to see another showing of Glitter. This is probably only going to be a one time offer, and a good one at that!

Call me when you can.

P.S. How are you coping with being where you are? The work conditions in your area, as far as I see on the news, seem horrendous. I hope you are doing okay though. Try to make the best of it. Are you using a face mask? Paper bag?

Talk soon,
John

-----Original Message-----
From: Tracy
To: John
Sent: 9/21/01
Subject: Curtains up!

Ladies and Gentlemen, Curtains up! I have great news for you Broadway lovers! I apologize for the timing of this email, I know that the short notice doesn't give you too much time to coordinate with others, but believe me this is worth it! By any chance are you interested in seeing an off-Broadway, a really fun, interactive, exciting, off-Broadway show tomorrow at 6:30? Oh, did I mention it's free? Yes, free!

With the unfortunate events that recently transpired in New York, the show needs to fill the theater because most of the audience who had purchased tickets cancelled after last week's events.

The show is called Tony N' Tina's Wedding. If you want or need any more information, details, or whatnot, you can visit their website and read all about it.

Hopefully you can make it, so if you can, please email me as soon as you know. Bring guests too, just be sure to supply me with the correct number of people. If you can get me this info by 2 p.m. tomorrow then all should be perfect.

I have to let you know though that there is a small possibility that the show might not go on at all.

I think that if no one, or very few people want to come even with the free tickets, then they will cancel the show. So try to get people to come. And also, it's a wedding so dress accordingly. This should be a fantastic night out on the town!

Hope to see you all there!
More later!
Hugs!
Tracy

* * *

From: John
To: Josh
Sent: 9/21/01
Subject: FW: It's On!

Charlie Casso

THE SHOW WILL GO ON! All of your tickets
have been secured and they are all at the box office of
the theater, just give them my name when you arrive.
Please arrive at 6:30 p.m. It's a wedding, so please get
to the church on time!

Let's meet at St. Luke's Church 308 West 46th
Street, closer to 8th Avenue.

There are 12 people on the list, but unfortunately a
few will probably be cancelling and others are a little
uncertain, so if you know anyone else who wants to
come but isn't included in your rsvp then please feel
free to bring them. As they say, the more the merrier!

Call me, email me, do whatever you need to contact
me if you have any Q's.
I'm at 212-XXX-XXXX until 5 p.m. and my cell is 917-
XXX-XXXX in case it's later.

Can't wait to see you! Hugs!
Tracy

* * *

"The show will go on" applies to Tony N' Tina's
Wedding probably just as much as it applies to any
of the other big Italian weddings I attend. How
many people can say they see bridesmaids wrestle
each other to the ground in attempts to get the
bouquet? At every wedding they attend? It's not
uncommon to hear, "I got the bouquet," followed
quickly by, "Yeah, but I got your earrings." It
happens.

I attend Tony N' Tina's Wedding in St. Luke's Church with Steven and Phoebe. The reception includes a sit-down dinner with a pot-smoking best man, a slutty bridesmaid, and an old maid. We heat up the dance floor to the chicken-dance, the electric side, and even the Macarena. The wedding transports me away from the situation outside, even if it's only for two hours.

The rationale for giving out free tickets stems from the notion it's better for a show to give away tickets and receive good word of mouth from audience members than to play to an empty theater. The recourse would be to give refunds to the few who paid for tickets and not have a show. This way some money can be made, word of mouth spread, and morale lifted for the actors. Unfortunately, the free tickets indicate things to come for Broadway. Attendance at many shows drops drastically following 9/11 and forces them to close.

True to themselves, New Yorkers and New York staples strive to succeed even when faced with devastation.

When John asks whether I use a face mask or a paper bag to help me breathe at work, he brings up a good point. We probably all should wear face masks at work, especially on the streets on the way to and from work. But we don't. And, by "we," I mean most of the people I observe, including, of course, myself. I fear years down the line I, along with many others, will have bronchial issues related to the air quality in the downtown area post 9/11.

Charlie Casso

Why aren't people wearing face masks, at least while they are in the downtown area? Everything looks yellow because of the debris in the air. People forgo the use of face masks though. I dress up for work because social norms mandate I must. Women still wear their heels to work, even though they had to kick off the ones they wore while traversing the Brooklyn Bridge mere days before, and men still wear their shiny loafers. But social norms have not adjusted for a post 9/11 world. Room doesn't get created for a new accessory, a face mask. Face masks may not be the most fashionable item. They may make me look like Michael Jackson, or worse, a nail salon employee, but the use of a face mask can probably help my lungs, at the very least. I can't say why Michael Jackson wears a face mask when he's out and about, but I'm pretty sure the reason nail salon employees (nail technicians?) wear masks is they don't want to breathe in dead skin cells while filing nails, or inhale too much acetate from nail polish. They protect themselves from inhaling dead skin cells and the like while, at this very moment, I breathe incinerated human, building, and plane parts. If people can be humble enough to file the garish, at times, toe nails of people while earning a pittance of a salary and still maintain enough dignity to protect their health, if not now then for the future, then people working in or around the WTC and Wall Street should have enough self-respect and self-esteem to do the same.

* * *

From: Michelle
To: Josh
Sent: 9/24/01
Subject: Calendar

Josh,

Well, looks like we have good news all around. First and foremost, thank you for all of the attention that you've given to us, particularly me, during this time when you are probably being pulled in about a million and one different directions. I really can't imagine how you are doing it. I received the calendar you sent and believe me, it's such a relief. Now I can plan our complete program (I hope) right away. You made it a lot easier, many thanks.

And regarding thanks, Josh, you definitely don't have to thank me for anything. I'm just relieved that you are all right. Events like 9/11, as unfortunate as they are, make the world a smaller place.

Michelle

* * *

Very true, events like this make the world a smaller place. John always says, "The only time the human race was ever nice to each other was right after September 11th." People hold doors open for each other, smile, *genuinely* smile, and are even friendly towards each other. People I come across act as if everyone knows each other. The reality is, as different as everyone is, we finally have something in common. We have shared a tragic experience together and it has brought us closer together, even if only for a moment.

I see *Don't Say a Word* at the AMC Lincoln Square movie theater with Steven and Phoebe. After the movie, we stroll around Times Square. American images emblazon Times Square, and we notice an adorable, cherubic-faced, twenty-something, black girl, with the biggest brown eyes I have ever seen, as she looks in a card shop window at the same time as us. An American flag sticks through and pokes out of her hairdo. We smile at each other and wish each other a good night, in a moment of New York camaraderie. How often had complete strangers exchanged pleasantries before 9/11?

Going Down and Moving On

Chapter Ten: Work Attempts to Make Stress Manageable

From: Cecile
To: All
Sent: 9/24/01
Subject: Potluck Luncheon

The New York office will host a "Potluck Luncheon" on October 5th at 12:30 p.m. Everyone is encouraged to participate. Consider bringing comfort food, an ethnic entrée, a snappy salad, or a delicious dessert. Make sure you bring your appetite. This should be a moment for everyone to come together, share a meal, relax, and enjoy. Additionally, if you fear you have limited culinary skills, feel at liberty to bring a store-bought dessert. In addition to all of the employee potluck offerings, SYNERGY is contributing the beverages for our potluck luncheon.

Once again, the "Potluck Luncheon" will take place on October 5th at 12:30 p.m.

Can't wait to see you there.

Thank you,
Cecile
Director of Human Resources

* * *

"Hey," Phoebe answers the phone.

"Josh, are you laughing?" she starts laughing as well because I cannot reply to her other than with more laughter and the few tears that spring from my eyes and roll down my cheeks.

"Ethnic entrées," I laugh-speak, "Cecile wants ethnic entrées."

"Cecile wants what?"

"Check your email," I say as I try to calm down.

"Okay, I'll check right now. Potluck luncheon... consider bringing..." Phoebe's voice rises along with her laughter, and mine, as she gets to "ethnic entrée" and "snappy salad."

"What is she smoking?" Phoebe asks.

"I have no clue, but I've never seen her send, or even say, anything like this before. Are we just punchy today?"

"No, Josh, this is legitimately hysterical. God, I can only imagine what you're going to bring."

"Whether it's collared greens, chicken parm, or corned beef, you'll eat it and you'll like it."

"You'll eat it and like it? Isn't that what they normally say to you?" Phoebe responds.

"Classy, Phoebe, real classy."

"Maybe I'll bring a tossed salad. You like your salad tossed, right?"

"Did you hear that?" I ask. "I just vomited a little. Kind of gross, Phoebe."

"I try."

"You succeed. What do you know about tossed salads anyway?"

"What," Phoebe protests, "you think only the gays know about tossed salads? Honey, us breeders invented tossed salads."

"And you know this... ahh, look at you, all prim and proper on the streets but in the bedroom, however, Phoebe, I'd have never guessed. You should ask Cecile if she would like a tossed salad."

"Has Steven tossed your salad?"

"I've never!"

"Really, Josh, because you look like you have."

In my head, I ask, "Do I really look like I have?"

Picking up on my silence, Phoebe immediately responds, "Josh, you know you have that innocent look to you, I'm just messing with you."

"Oh," I exhale, "whew."

"Or am I?" Phoebe taunts.

"Back to work you, you're too much," I say and laugh my way off the phone.

* * *

From: Cecile
To: All
Sent: 9/26/01
Subject: Mental Health

It's evident there are a fair number of you who are feeling the effects of 9/11 to this day. In an effort to make things more manageable for you, I want you to be aware of the resources that are available for you, to help you in this time of need. There are a number of symptoms that foretell of what the Department of Mental Health refers to as "Post Traumatic Stress Syndrome" (PTSS). These symptoms include, but are not limited to, feeling anxiety, having a loss of appetite or an inability to keep food down, fear, and having nightmares, whether repeated or not.

In an effort to help anyone who has PTSS, or anyone who thinks they may have PTSS, the Mental Health Association of New York City has set up mental health hot lines you may call. Experienced counselors are available to help anyone who needs or wants help. In addition, the counselors can make referrals should you need additional help. I strongly urge anyone who has any of the aforementioned symptoms to make use of these mental health hot lines.

Please make not of the following phone numbers:
For English speaking people: 877/(deleted)
For Asian speaking people: 877/(deleted)
For Spanish speaking people: 877/(deleted)

Should you have any questions or concerns, please do not hesitate to contact me. Your mental well-being should be the top priority.

If further information is needed, please contact me.

Thank you,
Cecile
Director of Human Resources

* * *

I call for help. I call three or four doctors and only receive the voicemail for each. I leave a message on each voicemail, but I receive not a single reply. The typo in her email where she writes, "Please make not of the following phone numbers," appears not to have been a typo, but rather a judgment on their effectiveness. So much for getting help. I understand a surge of people currently vie to meet with them. The lack of response, however, reinforces my "well, you can handle it yourself" mentality. Handle it myself I do. Not with drugs or anything, I actually have never done any drugs. I've never even smoked a cigarette. So when I say I handle it myself, I basically mean I just deal with it. I generally have a positive, upbeat attitude, and when things get to me they usually only get me down, if at all, for just a day or so.

These days are akin to bloodlettings. When I feel down, whether it is over something major or just the buildup, over time, of a myriad of minor things, I will hunker down somewhere, typically in my bedroom, and just stay to myself and possibly cry it out. Following September 11th, I have one of those days.

Seeing what happened, firsthand, on September 11th, however, doesn't have the same impact as a breakup or a combination of small events and, as a result, I worry about the longer-term effects. Will I always have nightmares about what happened? Will I have flashbacks for years and years to come like Vietnam veterans? Some of these thoughts cross my mind, and rightfully so. For these reasons, I reach out. But ultimately, yes, I must handle it myself.

From: Cecile
To: All
Sent: 9/26/01
Subject: Disturbing Forwards

A number of you have been sending forwards to your co-workers with unprofessional, and somewhat disturbing, content. These e-mails consist primarily of pictures taken from the WTC. Please be mindful that we have a great number of employees who either have lost family members on September 11th or who are still missing family members as a result of September 11th. These employees do not need to be reminded of the incident. I am sure you do not realize the impact the e-mails may have on others, and this is why I bring it to your attention at this time.

Remember, there are also a great number of employees who may not have lost someone but who may still be coping with PTSS. The e-mails, combined with the constant news and media coverage everyone is exposed to, may be doing psychological harm to these employees. So, if we must be inundated with coverage of the events via the media and news, please let that be it.

Thank you,
Cecile
Director of Human Resources

* * *

People send emails with disturbing content, one of which includes supposed pictures from a camera found at the WTC. One picture captures a close-up of a plane swooping in toward the photographer. Even if such a picture had been taken, the camera would have had to survive the impact, someone would have had to find the camera, develop the pictures, et cetera, et cetera. The fact someone could fabricate such pictures and claims stuns me. Additionally, those who knowingly forward such emails dismay me, especially since I receive them while at work, from co-workers.

I find relief in Cecile's email, as she attempts to thwart those sending out emails of a harrowing nature. I pray the people forwarding these emails don't believe everything they read as this level of naivete hopefully does not exist. Another viable way to explain the forwards maintains that forwarded email happens as a result of an employee's ennui at work.

The email Cecile mentions gets deleted from my computer when I receive it. It conveys such a sense of negativity I find myself compelled to delete it immediately. Life is short enough, as September 11th reminds me, without negativity. When I remove the sources of negativity in my life, I can keep a bright outlook on life. It's really only doom and gloom if I allow it to occur.

* * *

From: Josh
To: Phoebe
Sent: 9/27/01
Subject: Booked!

Guess what? I booked my hotel for my New Orleans trip this morning. WooHoo!!! HeeYay!! :O) I think above and beyond everything else, the thing that makes me the happiest about this right now is that I made a decision. Oh, and I had one of those black and white cookies from the corner store over here this morning. (It was really good too, very tasty.) Did you know that I called up a couple of the hotels this morning, even ones I didn't want, and found a lot of them are booked solid for that weekend? I guess a lot of people do go there around Halloween time. :O) :O)

Josh

* * *

From: Phoebe
To: Josh
Sent: 9/27/01
Subject: Re: Booked!

See? I knew they would be packed. You're lucky you found a room. Halloween time there gets packed. When I was there I wasn't in a hotel but the streets were beyond crowded. Another perk of going around that time is the temperature drops enough that it's bearable. Don't get me wrong, it's still hot and sticky, but it's better to go in October than say June, July, or God forbid August. And don't forget what I told you about rainy season there. It's approaching and boy, if you have never experienced a rainy season in New Orleans, well let's just say I'd hate to experience a hurricane in NOLA. Speaking of hurricanes, please, please, please bring me back some Hurricane mix from Pat O'Brien's. Hurricanes are the most amazing, knock you on your ass drinks ever. They taste like fruit punch, it's like sugar going right down your throat. You'll love it!

Ugggh, save me from meeting with Lynette, Ryan, and Shannon. They are going to go all NYPD on me, grilling me about sales numbers, who I contacted, how I contacted them, when, how often, who is left, what the plans are, on and on. I am going to fold under pressure. Our boss, Lynette, I can handle, but HER boss Ryan, the combination of the two of them whelms me. They want, want, want. I'm not an idea factory like you. I don't have new ideas for how to get the revenue in that they want. Ryan wants an idea factory, but that's not me. Try as I might, it takes me a while to develop a good plan. And even with all the time in the world, there just hasn't been any revenue coming in at all lately. Ultimately, that's all they care about – revenue, money. Uggh, I can feel the beads of sweat forming at the back of my neck right now. They'll roll down my back, and give me a chill right in the middle of my meeting. Then I'm going to have this odder than odd expression of cringe meets pain and they are going to wonder what the heck is wrong with me. And whatever their assumptions are, well I'm sure they won't be too far off. But that's okay. I just need to calm down and not have so much anxiety over this. Lynette knows how I get, so she already told me he would try to help me if / when she sees me sinking. I told her to try,

try, try as she might but if I can't be saved, hey thanks for trying. Just think of me as Phoebe, hamster in a wheel. Watch me as I exert all my energy trying and trying to get this money in, but instead I just go round and round, getting nowhere and getting there fast!

* * *

"Are you calling to say you'll go into the meeting for me?" Phoebe asks.

"Listen, hamster girl, first of all you can't be a hamster, you know how I hate rodents. I would never hang out with you if you were even remotely like a hamster. Secondly, you survived 9/11 here, at this very office, and you're worried about a meeting? If that doesn't give you perspective I don't know what will."

"Point taken. I'll try."

"It's do or do not, there is no try."

"Oh, God, it really is over, you're quoting *Star Wars*."

"Really? I haven't seen that movie since I was like six years old. Go figure."

"By the way, I was going to send you some info from the APA, before you look at it and ask why I'm sending you spam," Phoebe tells me.

I respond, "What's the APA?"

"American Psychological Association. They have a bunch of strategies for dealing with traumatic events. I know we haven't talked much about it, insert the sappy music here, but even if you feel fine now you may have a different reaction to what happened later."

"Oddly touching of you, and not in a creepy-Uncle kind of way. How did you come across the info?" I ask.

"I'm not going to say it doesn't get me down when I have time to think. I figure it's better to know what to expect and how to deal with things should they get worse."

"Fair enough. Good idea, Phoebe and, seriously, very touching. Actually, I haven't felt so touched since that time the priests asked me to stay after school and…"

"There's a special place in hell for you…"

I break back in, "That's what the nuns would say! But they watched, so what gives?"

"Apparently you do," Phoebe replies.

"Well-played, Phoebe, well-played."

"Back to what I was saying, just a heads up, and this applies to both of us, apparently when it comes to relationships there are loads of issues with feelings becoming unpredictable, intense, volatile, you name it. We'd better stay on our toes."

"I'd rather be on my back, but all right, toes it is. Damn terrorists, ruining all our fun."

Phoebe sees or just knows something's wrong. Maybe she feels the same way I do. She, too, might suffer from nightmares. Either way, intuition is one of the greatest assets a person has to help him or her have an effect on another. If Phoebe intuitively or subconsciously knows she should forward information to me that could help me to deal with issues I haven't yet discussed with her, that's evidence of a higher level of connection with and to the world.

Chapter Eleven: Work Fails at Chapter Ten: Sends Employees off Deep End.

From: Phoebe
To: Josh
Sent: 9/27/01
Subject: Really??

So, yeah, about the bomb squad, Josh… you think you could have mentioned the bomb scare when we talked before? I had no idea there was a bomb scare. What's worse is the fact that they didn't notify anyone... well, not anyone, they did notify some people, but that's the worst of it. Why mention it to some people and not others? Who is deciding who's valuable or worth saving and who isn't? I don't get it and I don't know if I even want to try to understand it. Furthermore, if they want to say they were trying to avoid a panic scare, I say bull! Panic-schmanic! As if we aren't all panic stricken enough just being here and having been through what we've been through. You know what else, they could've just made something up. They could've said they had to change the filters or something and they wanted us out of the building for twenty minutes or so. We would've left, no harm, no panic, and all would have been well. Now I'm just so mad I could… AAAAAGGGGGHHHHHH!!!

* * *

From: Josh
To: Steven
Sent: 9/27/01
Subject: uggh

Hey,

There was a bomb-scare here today-- the bomb-squad arrived and everything. But, you know, I had no idea. Some people from our office left, the whole rest of the building left, not me, or the people on my side of the office though. What the heck is that all about? Arrgh. They didn't make an announcement to evacuate, yet they had the bomb-squad arrive?
I'm still in one piece, but a little arrgh...
See you later.

Josh

* * *

From: Steven
To: Josh
Sent: 9/27/01
Subject: RE: uggh

Wow, that's definitely depravity at its worst, I must say. I'm sorry you have to be there. Chin up though, all will get better. In the meantime though, can you pants someone in management to make up for it? Kidding. Maybe you could follow senior management into the bathroom, wait till he's in a stall, and then scream "booooomb!!!" Kidding again, that isn't even funny. I just feel bad they did that. God forbid something did happen, that there really was a bomb or something, that's just an awful way for management to handle such a situation. You definitely should have been informed, as should everyone who works in your office. Once again, chin up. All will turn around (bright eyes).

Samooches!

* * *

No, I cannot not put my frustration into words, hence the "arrgh!" How do I find out about the bomb-scare? Easy: a co-worker asks me why he didn't see me outside when the bomb squad arrived. My reaction, of course, is to ask, "What bomb scare?" Apparently, a bomb threat has been phoned in to our office, along the lines of a plain and simple, "There's a bomb under one of the desk-chairs in your office. This is not a joke. Run." The recipient of the bomb threat informs management. Management, in-turn, phones the authorities. Management then proceeds to vacate the building, and takes with them only a select few, in order to not create "panic." I'm not the lone, slightly agitated employee left out of the evacuation, however, as evidenced by Phoebe's panic-schmanic, angst-ridden email.

* * *

From: Josh
To: John
Sent: 09/27/01
Subject: Hey

So, there was a bomb-scare here today. It seems all of the other floors evacuated, including half of this one. Not I, nor a bunch of the other people in here. It seems they don't make announcements to evacuate. They call the bomb-squad, which shows up and all, but the building people don't want to panic everyone. Excuse me if I'm wrong, but I think this is quite similar to the people who made the announcements in the WTC which stated something to the effect of "go back to your desks--remain in your offices." They didn't want people to evacuate or panic etc. They advised them to remain where they were. It's like come on, better safe than sorry. Your friend is so lucky that his office rented space somewhere else. Arrgh.

On a happy, I-have-to-get-away-from-here kind of note, I booked my hotel for New Orleans this morning. Yee-hah!!!

Till later,
Josh

* * *

From: John
To: Josh
Sent: 9/27/01
Subject: Re: Hey

Bet that makes you feel real good about being back at work, now doesn't it? Your boss should raise hell with the building manager over there and find out why not everyone was informed. (I'm assuming that this was a building manager error. Please say it wasn't someone who actually works with you who didn't give the heads up to everyone.) Is this really the land of opportunity or...?

* * *

Since Steven and I are still somewhat new to each other, there's comfort in contacting John. He knows me well enough I can air my frustrations with him. If I want to be sadomasochistic, I can consider contacting Drug-addled Ex. No way, no how though, as I imagine the following scenario would unfold:

"You'll never believe what happened. Some pill-head phoned in a bomb threat at work and..."

"Pill? What pills? Where?"

"Good grief."

Click.

In my email to John, I express my frustrations more clearly. The requisite "arrgh" remains, but I convey what vexes me so much about the bomb scare. I should be given the choice to evacuate or stay in the event of a bomb scare. Management should not keep me in the dark about life-threatening situations that affect me. While I air my vexations with friends, others who work for the company choose to air their frustrations in a slightly different manner.

* * *

From: Anonymous
To: All
Sent: 9/28/01
Subject: Bomb Scare: Pussy

Bomb Scare: Pussy

Main Entry: pus·sy
Pronunciation: puhs-ee
Function: noun
Etymology: 1875-80 Dutch diminutive of poes vulva
Date: 19th century

Meaning: an ineffectual or timid person

Eg. Rather than ensuring the safety of all Synergy employees, or even just warning the employees about the bomb scare, the management team left the building yesterday like a bunch of pussies.

* * *

Ballsy? I think so. It isn't me who sends this email. (Just to clarify.) The email is sent from "Anonymous," whoever that is. I sincerely don't know who the real author of the email is. I do know he or she must be quite technologically savvy to get his or her name to appear as "Anonymous" or to have created some weird email address that can attach itself to the company's email system.

* * *

From: Peter
To: All
Sent: 9/28/01
Subject: Re: Bomb Scare: Cowardice

How dare you say that what management did was timid, when you send out an email anonymously!

* * *

As for why this Peter, whose name is synonymous with the type of person he's being, stands up for the company I will never understand. I don't know Peter. He must work in a satellite office overseas.

* * *

From: Ryan
To: All
Sent: 9/28/01
Subject: Re:Bomb Scare: Pussy

To Synergy staff

    A pussy is exactly what "Anonymous" is being. If you have a conviction, then stand by it. If any employee wants to talk about the events that transpired yesterday, then stand up and say so. I will make myself available in order to discuss these matters the way that they should be; not through a pussy email, and certainly not in response to such a pussy email as the one sent by "Anonymous." What happened yesterday, that is being referred to as a "bomb scare" is what we deemed to be a minor incident that we firmly believe was handled correctly and in the best interest of everyone involved. Whatever is done, whether it is on my part alone, or on the part of any of my managers here, is done with your best interest at heart. It's a shame that in our midst, in contrast to myself and the managers here, we have a spineless pussy who not only doesn't see the merit in what we did but who also won't say it to our faces without using an alias.

    With September 11th shadowing our every thought, we seek to provide our employees with a safe place of work. The reports that were circulating yesterday about a threat to our safety here needed to be investigated before we alarmed our staff. We felt it right to investigate first, see what threat there actually was, and then inform. We stand by our decisions. Anyone who would like to discuss these issues further is invited to do so with me. I will make myself available in the conference room today at noon.

As for the spineless employee who dares to endanger the morale of the staff by questioning the tactics employed by management in the best interest of the staff, I can only relay to you my sheer and utter disappointment in your pitiful sense of self and of this company.

Ryan

* * *

"He can't be serious," Lynette says to me without making eye contact. She nods her head in the direction of Ryan's office. Ryan stands in the doorframe of his office, arms crossed in front of his chest, as he peers across the rows of cubicles. Lynette searches for something in the inbox at her desk as she continues, "He can't really think the person who sent that email will meet with him to discuss it. It's all for show."

The slam of a door sounds. The red numbers on my digital clock read 11:54 a.m. Heavy footsteps make their way across the office floor, slowly, forcefully, and authoritatively. Ryan stares straight ahead as he plods his way across the office toward the glass-walled conference room. He approaches the glass doors. He stops, turns around, and gives his best blue steel look as if to warn anyone who might attend the conference that he is ready. Ryan opens the conference room door, enters, and plants himself in a high-backed leather chair.

Lynette stands up in her cubicle and pretends she has to get something, but in reality she checks to see if Ryan remains in the conference room. Since my cubicle shares a wall with hers, and she is clearly aggravated by his pompous act of machismo, she comments under her breath, "He wants everyone to see how big his balls are. He makes me sick."

The numbers on the clock now read 11:59 a.m. Ryan remains alone in the room. The girl from accounting walks toward the office. Lynette's eyes follow her movements, as do mine. She can't really be going to meet Ryan for the discussion, can she? She turns into the cubicle on her right. She must need to speak with the person in charge of billing. Close call.

The clock now reads 12:05 p.m. and Ryan remains the lone wolf in the conference room. Two more minutes tick by and Ryan, hands on hips, chest puffed out, finally emerges from the room. Management never again broaches the subject of the bomb scare.

I take a second to forward Ryan's email to Steven. All I write in my email is, "Steven, This is the president of our company's response..." At the same time, employees start to weigh in on the issues at hand as well.

* * *

From: Steven
To: Josh
Sent: 9/28/01
Subject: Re: Re:Bomb Scare: Pussy

Well, it may be that it required all of the management to check out if the bomb scare was real or not. But the fact that they shared no information with employees is horrible. What they did may be defensible, but what they didn't do is inexcusable. We just had our emergency procedures meeting, where we went over every conceivable calamity, and what the response should be. It was pointed out that when there is a fire, or bomb, or bomb threat, the normal procedure is to evacuate two floors down, two floors up, and not tell the other floors. Our VP said if there is ever a bomb threat, she would tell us, and have us evacuate at our own discretion. She said, "It's your life you need to make your own decision." The biggest point of contention at the meeting was over the evacuation drill that we're having next week. Most of the employees want to do a full run through, go down all 19 flights of stairs, whereas the building management only wants to do a three-floor run through. I think you need to round up your friends and go to that meeting and raise your concerns. From what you tell me it sounds like your management does not take its employees' health and well being seriously.

* * *

From: Nadine
To: Peter; Anonymous
CC: All
Sent: 9/28/01
Subject: Re: Bomb Scare: Pussy

I don't know how much any of you know about e-mail systems, but it's not anonymous. Your e-mail address attached and went out to the entire company.

Also, the most important thing in any crisis situation is to calmly get yourself to safety. We're all adults, and need to take responsibility for our own safety in any critical situation. I for one would be offended if there were people hanging back to save me. I'll get myself out, help anyone who NEEDS help, and be thankful that I had an opportunity to evacuate the building.

Thank you,
Nadine Gerber
Graphic Designer
713.XXX.XXXX

* * *

It's easy for Nadine to say we need to take responsibility for our own safety and she would be offended if people were hanging back to save her. She has no idea what has been going on here in the New York office. Nadine, with her 713 area code, lives a comfortable distance from the employees who had to run from work on 9/11, only to return to an area that looks like a full-blown war zone, breathe in the most putrid and vile smelling air on a daily basis, and have bosses breathe down our necks in order to get money in to keep the magazines alive. I must cope with the fact in the event of bomb scare I will not be warned, because my priority, to "get the money in," trumps all. That, excuse my Brooklyn-English, cocksucker, has no idea. None. It must be nice in area code 713. 713 must also be a good place to brown-nose from. It's Texas, which is about half the country away from the New York office, but I'm quite sure her experience has been the same as mine.

My response, should I not be smart enough to keep out of it, would read something like this:

Charlie Casso

Re: Nadine the brown-nose, here's a word for you.

Main Entry: syc·co·phant
Pronunciation: sih-keh-fent
Function: noun
Etymology: Started in the time of the caveman
when suck-ups would do their best to make sure that
someone else gave them their grog, and/or leg of
pterodactyl.
Meaning: a servile, self-seeking, flatterer who pisses
off everyone else in the process.

Eg. When someone lives far enough away
from a tragic, mind-and-life-altering event, yet
has the audacity to comment on it in a way
which serves to belittle the fears of others while,
at the same time, tries to appease and assuage the
egos of the bigwigs, that someone, nay, cunt,
earns her status as a sycophant.

If you would like to further increase your
vocabulary, Nadine dearest, I would be more
than glad to offer you two more words; they are
small though, but I'm sure you can guess what
they are.

* * *

From: Anna
To: All
Sent: 9/28/01
Subject: email

I have had some calls and responses to the disturbing email that went out today, supposedly from me.

I would like to clarify that it was not me, as I hope was apparent from its nature.

Anna
Synergy

* * *

From: Alan
To: All
Sent: 9/28/01
Subject: Re: Bomb Scare: Pussy

This email is being sent to clarify the origin of the email titled "Bomb Scare: Pussy." We would like to say that the email was NOT SENT from Anna. We are making the investigation of the source of that email a top priority.

Alan
Manager, Computer Technology
Synergy

* * *

Whether it was Anna or not, it doesn't really matter. I'm just glad someone sent that email. It's reassuring to see Steven's office handles situations such as bomb scares tactfully. Now that my frustration about the bomb scare is off my chest maybe it'll be a bit easier to breathe around here.

Chapter Twelve: If the Air Was Really That Bad You Wouldn't Be Able to Complain about Receiving Anthrax in the Mail.

From: Cecile
To: All
Sent: 10/1/01
Subject: RE: Air Quality

   To everyone at the NYC office: A number you have inquired about the smell of "something burning." What you smell comes from the fires that are still burning at the WTC site.
Depending on the direction and intensity the wind, the smell proportionately increases/decreases.
   Building Management has changed all filters both inside and rooftop. They continue to monitor the internal air quality. As people enter the building any outside smell will also follow them in. As the elevators go up and down they too push the smell to all floors. Building management is doing what it can to minimize outside smells from coming into the building.

If you have any questions please contact me.

Thank you,
Cecile
Director of Human Resources

                         * * *

   "How are you holding up in your cubicle over there?" I ask as I pick up the phone.

"Eh," Phoebe responds, "as good as can be expected under the circumstances. I actually taste ash."

"You used to smoke, didn't you?"

"Not the same, Josh. Although, if I'm going to feel the effects of smoking I may very well take it up again."

"Please don't even joke about that. You'd be a bad smoker, I can tell. I can see you tossing your cigarette butt and it landing on someone."

"So funny I forgot to laugh. I'm not that vapid. You never dated a smoker, right?"

"Hello, Drug-addled Ex was a smoker."

"Get out!"

"Seriously. During out first conversation I asked him if he smoked or did any drugs. He said no to both. Over time, on the other hand..."

"I can't imagine you with a smoker."

"I know, but if you like someone, or start to like someone, I guess you overlook some things."

"Yeah," Phoebe agrees. "And how'd that work out for ya?"

"For someone who can't breathe you certainly manage to talk a lot."

"Sorry, low blow. How are you holding up over there?"

"Same. I'd say we should go out for an early lunch today but it's not like it's any better outside."

Building management may have changed the filters but they definitely need to change them again. Hourly. So much dirt and soot pervade the air that it becomes impossible for filters to really clean the air without constant replacement.

* * *

From: Cecile
To: All
Sent: 10/5/01
Subject: Memorial Service

For anyone who would like to attend, a memorial service is being held for Ryan's brother on Saturday, October 13th. The exact details regarding the time and location will be sent to those of you who express interest in attending.

If you would like further information, please give me a call.

Thank you,
Cecile
Director of Human Resources

* * *

Although I one hundred percent empathize with Ryan for his loss, going to the memorial service would be too much for me to handle. I'm sure it would be nice of me to go though. Steven occupies my free thoughts right now. I decide to give him a call and, while the phone rings, I try to muster up something to say.

"Morning, handsome," I begin.

"Back at you, gorgeous."

"Wondering if you have some free time later today."

"Actually," he begins, as I realize this won't be good, "I have plans to go over a friend's tonight. Just a low-key night, probably watch a movie and relax. I have to send you an invite for a friend's birthday party by the way."

"Are these your pot-smoker friends?"

"Does it matter?"

"I'll take that as a yes," I respond. "It's just I don't want to see you falling into all of that. I've had some bad experiences with people who were addicted…"

"It just takes the edge off, that's all. You have absolutely nothing to be worried about, I promise you."

The silence on my end of the line is met with his response, "Man, I need to get these emails sent pronto. Gotta run. Talk later."

Going Down and Moving On

Our contact with each wanes, on both sides. Emails become less frequent, as do phone calls. Work usurps my time. Management wears the carpet to a new low, as pacing between the rows of cubicles hits an all time high. Strained looks adorn the faces of those in charge. Management may be the first on the chopping block because of their high salaries, but, while they remain, they threaten me with discerning glares, seething for money.

* * *

From: Steven
To: Josh
Sent: 10/8/01
Subject: Re: :0)
Hey Sexy,

Sorry to cut you off this morning, mucho busy... then I realized I lost your work number. Here is the email I told you about...
-----Original Message-----
Sent: Thursday, October 04, 2001
Subject: Join me for a celebration!

As I have spent the past few weeks trying to cope with our new reality, I have also struggled with the fact that my birthday is fast approaching. What was so important to me during the days and months before September 11th seems so insignificant now. In the days and weeks since, on the rare instance that my birthday entered my mind I quickly turned my thoughts away from it. I couldn't bare the thought of any kind of celebration. Well, with a little encouragement from my family and friends, I have decided that a gathering would be not just warranted but necessary.

What would make me happy would be for all of my friends and loved ones to share the moment with me. All I need is to be surrounded by love, admiration, positivity and a sense of belonging. Yes, I am turning another year older and would love for you to spend the evening with me. Please join me at the Starlight Bar & Lounge on Saturday, October 20th at 9:00 PM.

Starlight Bar & Lounge 167 Avenue A (between 10th and 11th)

Please RSVP to me and let me know if you will be bringing a guest before October 19th. I will be providing the doorman with a guest list to guarantee that everyone gets in and does not have to pay a cover.

* * *

I require, at this point, more than "sorry to cut you off" and a forwarded invite to a birthday party. Nevermind the "lost your work number" part. What happened to the Summer of Love Redux? What happened to my pre-9/11, post-Drug-addled Boyfriend world? What I wouldn't give to breathe freely right now.

* * *

From: Cecile
To: All
Sent: 10/15/01
Subject: Internal Air Quality

I've informed building management of the poor
internal air quality and have asked them to take the
necessary steps to mitigate the problem.

Thank you,
Cecile
Director of Human Resources

* * *

I am more than certain irreversible damage has
been done to the lungs and well being of many of
the employees in the New York office. On the bright
side, however, I really don't have too much cause
for complaint in that at least I'm alive. Things could
be much worse and I should definitively and
conclusively count myself among the lucky ones.

* * *

From: Cecile
To: All
Sent: 10/15/01
Subject: Latex Disposal Gloves

If you have concerns about opening your mail due
to the recent anthrax threats, you can pick-up a pair of
latex disposable gloves at the receptionist.

Thank you,
Cecile
Director of Human Resources

* * *

Between my relationship with Steven, bomb threats, the air quality at work, and now the threat of anthrax in the mail, things have to bottom out soon. The receptionist, who normally freaks out over every little thing, opens a letter addressed to the magazine and out flies a white powdery substance. She leaps out of her chair and tears through the office toward the bathroom, as high-pitched screams of "Oh my God" echo in her wake. The business communications I receive must now be inspected carefully, and the same goes for my personal communications as my relationship with Steven disintegrates pretty darn quickly. I feel, as I also believe he feels, 9/11 adversely impacts our relationship.

After 9/11, two types of people exist in my world: the people who deal with it big time (those who lost family members and loved ones) and those who deal with it on a somewhat lesser, yet not insignificant, level. I think of myself as being in the latter part. I went through it, felt it literally, saw it literally, and have to deal with the repercussions. I do not complain. I don't scream, shout, or compare my grief to the grief felt by anyone else.

So, when others wax poetic about their horrific experiences, when they were miles away, it perturbs me. I think: if I don't complain about it then why should they? If I keep my feelings bottled up, why can't they? A divide forms between us, as Steven becomes dark and moody. One minute I feel passion, another ambivalence. I tell him I think I love him in the Union Square train station as we say our goodbyes for the night. A normal person would question "Who does that," while a normal New Yorker would simply say "I'd do that" or "I could see doing that." At the end of a date, as we hug goodbye in the subway station, right before we each head to our respective subway platforms, I feel the pull I feel in my heart when I love someone and being away from them is going to hurt. I say, "I, umm, I think I love you," in a very out of the blue, very matter of fact, very, "Okay, now I'm going to go get my train because I don't want to wait for a response and I'm out on a limb here," kind of way. 9/11 propels me into a deeper attachment with Steven. In a time of tragedy, human nature makes me seek comfort in those around me. Life had been amazing up until then, and now times have changed.

* * *

From: Cecile
To: All
Sent: 10/16/01
Subject: Safety Alert: Anthrax Letter Handling

It has recently come to my attention that letters containing anthrax have been received in several states now. Anthrax is not contagious, so if someone in this office should become infected, it will not affect others in the office. In any event, I have compiled some guidelines to make our workplace a little safer and a little less scary. Should a letter containing anthrax, or a powdery substance, be received, please refer to this email in order to handle the situation appropriately.

1. When opening mail, until further notice, be sure to wear latex, disposable gloves. These can be found at the receptionist's desk.
2. Mere exposure to anthrax does not mean you will be infected. In order to be infected, you need to inhale anthrax spores or have anthrax spores enter your body through cuts on your skin. Keep in mind, the inhalation of these spores can be life-threatening, so exercise extreme caution when handling mail. Additionally, handling letters with gloves will alleviate some concern regarding exposure through the skin.
3. In the event that someone should become infected, immediately seek medical treatment. Should you receive a letter or a package, directed to your attention, which is marked with a threatening message or which seems to be leaking a powdery substance, DO NOT open the letter or

package. Immediately place the letter or package in a bag or container that can be either sealed or covered to prevent exposure of the contents to others. Once the suspicious letter or package has been contained, warn others of its presence and location and REPORT THE INCIDENT to the local police (and management if at work).

Also, police and/or management may require that you provide a list of all people who were in the area when the letter / package was discovered.

If you have any questions, please contact me.

Thank you,
Cecile
Director of Human Resources

Chapter Thirteen: Tick, Tick... Boom, indeed.

From: Steven
To: Josh
Sent: 10/16/01
Subject: be careful

Beware ... October 20th

Shower at your own risk on October 20th,
just don't say you weren't warned.

Reports from trusted sources indicate that, starting at dawn of the 20th, highly trained, venomous snakes will be released into the sewage system by a surly piper peeved at having recently been laid off from work. These snakes have been deprived clean water for weeks now, and will be slithering at accelerated speeds in search of such. They will snake their way up through the pipes and strike you from the drain at your feet once you are in the shower with the water running. It is recommended that all United States citizens refrain from showering on the 20th and until further notice. Once the snakes are contained, then citizens may resume showering as normal.

This information was conveyed from the council of pied pipers who relayed the news, in melody only, to a six year old boy, who in turn relayed it to his hard-of-hearing grandmother, who in turn called her daughter, but mistakenly dialed the wrong number and told a complete stranger who barely spoke English, who wrote it on the bathroom wall of the 7-11 in New Hyde Park, Long Island.

So, yes, it's totally true. Shower now, or don't shower at all.

Good luck and God bless.

* * *

I accompany Steven to an Off-Broadway Jonathan Larson play by the name of "tick, tick... Boom" which stars Molly Ringwald and Joey McIntyre. Before the show, Steven and I revisit a conversation I had with John earlier about how people complain about experiencing 9/11 even though they had been safe in their offices, far from the scene.

"Today was unbearable," Steven vents. "Our receptionist remains on sick leave. She hasn't been back since 9/11 and we all take turns covering for her, an hour apiece."

"Wait. Why doesn't your office hire a temp until she returns?"

"They don't have the money for it. The advertisers have all, well, mostly, pulled out. The income's not going to flow in for a while, so they're cutting every expense they can."

"Don't you hate it when people pull out? Okay, yes, I realize what I just said. You know what I mean. My God. What happened to the girl that she's still out of work? Was she in the WTC when it happened?"

"No. She was in the office where I work. 57th and Lex."

"Okay, color me confused. What happened there? What happened at your office that got to her?"

"Well, she saw everything on the news. We had the TVs on and watched as everything unfolded."

"Are you seriously telling me she got so traumatized watching the news? From miles away?"

"Just because she wasn't there doesn't make her experience less traumatic than anyone else's."

"Yeah, it does. Steven, she watched it on TV. Out of work, for weeks, because she watched what happened on TV? That's the same as the people who were in the WTC, who ran down the stairs, who fled for their lives?"

"Yes. Josh, there's no difference, and I can't believe you can distinguish between the two."

Steven feels people, regardless of how far they were from the WTC on 9/11, have just as much right to complain as anyone else. I don't feel the same. I want to complain, I want to scream, but my calls for help all go to voicemail. As such, I don't want to hear about the plight of others while mine own goes unvoiced.

The conversation deepens the ravine between us.

With a handful of days to go before Halloween hits, we arrange to meet at St. Mark's Church, in the little area outside adorned with benches and shaded by trees. We figure we'll see what we do from there. When we meet, we sit on a bench outside the church for a couple of minutes in silence. Uncomfortable silences happen to be only situationally uncomfortable, depending upon what broaches the silence. A talk about our relationship broaches our silence. Any talk about relationships becomes uncomfortable. These should be called uncomfortable utterances, or something of that sort, because I'd prefer the silence to the talk that ensues.

"So," Steven remarks.

I reply, "Sew buttons."

"You got me again."

"What are you thinking?"

"I'm thinking I'm confused. I'm very confused. It's like part of me tells me to stay because I like you. I have fun with you. There's something great here. But."

"But?"

"There's also something that tells me to go. There's too much going on right now. Dealing with 9/11, I feel like, I don't know. I just feel unsettled. Like I'm changing. I started smoking again. I don't know what my priorities are anymore."

"Oh."

"I know this is great and that's what's so confusing. Stay. Go. Stay or go. I can't figure it out."

I get on my feet as he follows suit. Arms outstretched, I hug him softly, weakly, and, on the median between shock and tears, utter, "Well, then go."

I feel the bit of doubt, the part that tells Steven to go, puts a permanent wound on my heart. The "I love NY" design floats in front of my eyes. The black spot, signifying a heart attack, slowly burns itself onto the heart. Similarly, I will go on even though I will always carry a trace of the impact with me.

Fresh on the heels of my break-up with Steven, I focus on my business trip to New Orleans. Maybe the trip can re-start things, similar to how Las Vegas rejuvenated me after my break-up with Drug-addled Boyfriend. The black town car picks me up at work to take me to JFK International Airport. The sun shines through the window and warms my arm. The sun's warmth reminds me that I still have the capacity to feel. Thankfully, upon arrival in NOLA, my eyes alight on the balconies in the French Quarter that don Halloween decorations and a bevy of flags, including the American flag and Gay Pride flag.

Charlie Casso

I take three clients out for dinner and drinks on Bourbon Street. They're all professional, in their 30s, and, of course, married. This tangential information, in appearance a non-sequitur, holds importance in terms of advertising and other such boys' club professions. It seems almost everyone in the industry is white, young-ish, and married. Part of my job tonight includes keeping conversation casual yet not so casual that it becomes personal because although they may suspect my affinity for those who hold the y chromosome, to talk about it would be another thing all together. We don't have much in common when it comes to our love lives. One of my clients resembles Patrick Swayze. Surely, he makes some lucky girl very happy. I take a second to daydream about what his extracurricular activities could include, as Patrick Swayze was, in his heyday, Patrick Swayze, and then I come back down from my happy place as I suppress my drool. The realization that my daydream is prescient creeps up on me, nay, it slaps me harder than most domestic violence incidents that involve frying pans, when the client grabs my wrist and pulls me into a gay pub on St. Ann Street.

Client asks, "What would you like?"

I remain in stunned silence as I wonder if he means a drink or something else when he interrupts with clarification, "Drink? What would you like to drink?"

I wonder how obvious I am, as I reply, "Oh, I knew that. Midori Sour." I don't even say thank you, I'm so caught off guard.

Client gets two drinks from the bar, my Midori Sour and his beer. Of course he drinks beer, after all, I did think he was straight only a few moments ago. Wait, on second thought, maybe he is straight and doesn't realize we're in a gay bar. Oh, damn. A wave of uneasiness strikes me. I feel like I have to go to the bathroom. God, this is like what horses must feel like when they get scared. I think they poo when they get scared. Way to go, Josh, I think to myself, real classy. Well, if he's straight, what's the worst that can happen? A black eye? I need to talk to him. The silence needs to end.

I ask him, "So, how's New Orleans been treating you so far?"

"Good. Could be better though."

In my head, I ask, "How so? Wondering where all the girls are?"

Out loud, I ask him, "How so?"

"Well for starters…" He puts his hand on the back of my neck and pulls me in for a kiss that would make the record playing scratch to a halt if this were a movie. A full minute elapses while his tongue searches the depths of my mouth. We become two separate beings again, and the music, once again, plays.

"That was unexpected," I admit. "I couldn't tell if you were gay or not."

"Well, can you tell now?" he asks, as he takes a swig of his beer. "I can show you how gay I am if you want. I'd really like to show you."

In my head, I say, "Sweet Jesus, you're hot."

Out loud, I say, "Sweet Jesus, you're hot."

In my head and out loud, in unison, I say, "Damn, I wasn't supposed to say that out loud."

When people defy my expectations, the effect becomes ethereal. I get a bit of the innocence I had in childhood back and I look at the world, even if just for a moment, with eyes wide open as if anything really is possible. Client makes me feel, once again, like anything is possible. A hunky, Patrick Swayze look-a-like, with a successful career and a tongue that could make nuns moan, rejuvenates me to a semblance of my pre-9/11 self. Thankfully, I have the whole weekend in NOLA ahead since I made sure to extend my trip. And, of course, I enjoy the time spent both with and without clients.

On Thursday night, October 25th, I walk into a bar on St. Ann and Bourbon Street and, while there, I notice a guy standing not too far away. We do not exchange any words or anything. He simply stands not too far away from me, and wears nice enough clothing. Nothing flashy, just a pair of blue jeans and a dark t-shirt.

The next evening, Friday the 26th, I stroll around the French Quarter on my way to Burgundy Street and see the same guy walk down the street. We each do a double take and I ask him if the direction I'm going in leads to Burgundy. I know for a fact I'm heading in the right direction, but I really want to talk to him and so I figure why not just pretend I need directions.

"Sorry, am I headed in the right direction?"

"Well, that depends on what you're looking for, now doesn't it?"

I think, "What I'm looking for would make sailors blush."

I say, "That would help, wouldn't it? I'm looking for Burgundy Street. Is it far from here?"

"Well, no, it's not far at all. It's just a few blocks from here. First you pass… and then…" As he gives me the most detailed directions imaginable, which include the names of the streets between St. Ann and Burgundy, I completely zone out. I focus on his full lips, his scruff, his eyes, everything, except his words. And then I realize, oh crap, he has stopped speaking. What do I say?

In a blatant attempt to get his mind on sex so he doesn't realize where my mind just went, I state, "I was thinking I'd head there to browse around, but I feel so hot and sweaty now. The weather's really sticky today, and I'm like wet all over. I'll make a quick trip to Burgundy then head to my hotel to take a shower and change."

His eyes glass over, the very same way mine must have, so I take advantage of the opportunity and thank him for the directions, give a smile both Baby June and Mama Rose would be proud of, and let each of us go our own ways. Afterwards, we each look back one last time and smile.

The following day, Saturday, I do not have work at all. Saturday is mine for the taking. I take complete advantage of my time and freedom. I visit a couple of cemeteries, browse the quaint art shops that bespeckle the quarter, eat more beignets, snack on some praline chasers, and, at night, I visit one of the bars on St. Ann and Bourbon Street. As I drink a Midori Sour by the bar, I look over to my right and find that directions guy stands about three feet away. I approach him and say, "Hey, directions guy" in a blunt, yes I just gave you the nickname "directions guy" kind of way. We can now finally have a conversation, and we realize we have seen each other now three days in a row. It's quite a coincidence since he hails from Baton Rouge and hardly ever comes to New Orleans and I come from New York and this marks my first trip.

We exit the under-lit and overcrowded bar and talk on the corner of St. Ann Street in the balmy night air of New Orleans.

"So, I have to ask," he says, "were you there, in New York, on September 11th?"

"Well, I work right by the World Trade Center," I begin. My office building literally trembled under my feet that morning." I sigh a deep, yet quick, sigh as my eyes glass over with the pain of seeing the events flash through my mind. My eyes dart away from him. Vulnerability, at this moment, makes me want to run. "Long story short, I was crossing the Brooklyn Bridge as the first tower collapsed. I made it though. I'm here."

"You live all the way in New York," he replies. "I can't let myself fall for you. Something tells me, though, that you're going to make it really hard for me not to."

Chapter Fourteen: Happy Halloween, Mister Officer

Upon my return to the New York office, I settle myself into work and ready myself for the day. My coffee sits on my desk, as does my fiesta bagel with fat free cream cheese, both untouched so far. I start to read my emails but Lynette interrupts me with a sense of urgency. She must speak with Phoebe and I, at once. Lynette quickly gathers us and starts the debriefing.

"Josh, Phoebe," she begins, "you know how the magazines are in a crunch for money right now, right?"

Phoebe and I nod quickly in agreement.

Lynette continues, "Ryan wants thirty thousand dollars of new ad revenue from us. Tomorrow, by five o'clock. He needs the insertion orders on his desk. That works out to ten thousand dollars worth of ad revenue from each of us, minimum. Drop everything else you have on your plates and get those insertion orders signed and on his desk."

Rising to the occasion, Phoebe and I respond, "Sure, you got it. No problem."

Phoebe and I move to return to our cubicles, but Lynette puts her hands on her temples as if she suffers from the onset of a migraine and exclaims, "Wait." She grimaces, but continues, "I didn't want to tell you this. I didn't want to scare you, but I think you need to know. I would want to know. Ryan wants the ad revenue in from us by tomorrow at five and he wants me to fire whoever here doesn't bring in his or her ten thousand dollars of revenue. If I don't bring in my ten thousand, Ryan will fire me. And he said if I don't fire either or both of you, should you not bring in the money, then he will fire me in your place. I have a husband, I have three children, and I have a house. I need my income. So, I hate to say it, but if I have to fire you I will. But I know I won't have to because we will all get that money in by five o'clock tomorrow. Call your biggest clients. Do not stop until you get the signed insertion orders signed and in your hands. Ten thousand each. All right? Let's do this."

Nothing motivates me to get the ad revenue in like the threat of termination. And nothing scares the proverbial crap out of me like that does. The last time I felt this way I got French-kissed against a wall, but where's my hot Patrick Swayze look-alike client now? I turn over every stone, not for him, unfortunately, but for the insertion orders. I call my top advertisers and urge them to increase their ad space or up-sell them to the back cover if they already have ads confirmed. I call every client I can think of, even the mom-and-pop clients like Randy and Michelle. I call, email, and fax clients ad nauseum until I achieve my goal. I raise a little over twelve thousand dollars by the allotted time, and have the contracts signed and in my hands too. I sell more than even Lynette, and thoroughly impress her. Phoebe, unfortunately, doesn't bring in as much revenue as Lynette or me, but the combined total for the three of gets us to our goal. Lynette, Phoebe, and I deliver the stack of signed insertion orders to Ryan's office. While he speaks on his telephone, he nods his head up at us to see what we want. Lynette waves her hand with the insertion orders to the left and right of her, to indicate all three of us had a part in the orders, and places the stack on the middle of his intimidating, over-sized redwood desk. With the termination threat debacle under our belts, we leave Ryan's office and release a sigh of relief.

* * *

From: Cecile
To: All
Sent: 10/30/01
Subject: Impromptu Office Party

Synergy would like to invite you to an impromptu office party to celebrate our successes in dealing with the recent events in the New York office.

Please make yourself available tonight to meet at Harry's Pub at 7 o'clock. Synergy will be funding the open bar event for all Synergy employees between seven and ten p.m.

This is an incredible opportunity to spend time with, and get to know and appreciate more deeply, our fellow co-workers.

If you have any questions, please contact me.

Thank you,
Cecile
Director of Human Resources

* * *

"It's a little weird to be out on a Tuesday like this, but, hey, whatever works," Phoebe shrugs.

I concur, "True, especially with Cecile here. I couldn't really imagine her at a bar, pub, whatnot, but there she stands. Really upright, too. How does she stand so straight?"

"What pisses me off is they can spend God knows how much on this, yet we had to bust our asses for the last two days or get canned. If they have money for this then why the pressure?"

"Beats me."

Out of the corner of my eye I notice a female co-worker, who has been known to drink during her lunch hour, leaving the men's room. "Phoebe, nine o'clock."

"I don't know what time it is, but I don't think it's nine."

"No, fool," I reply, "look," as I nod in the direction of the men's room.

"Did Drunksie the Clown just come out of the men's room?"

"Yes, and her hair is all tousled."

"Dirty blondes have all the fun."

"No, *really* dirty blondes have all the fun,"

As the door to the men's room opens once more, and Ryan walks out, Phoebe faces me with the revelation, "Ryan and Drunksie?"

"That's what it looks like."

"I did not see that coming."

"Let's hope she did," I reply.

"Well, you gotta hand it to her, for someone who drinks during lunch and falls asleep at her desk, at least she's lucid enough to know what to do to keep her job."

"Cheers, to Drunksie," I offer as I raise my glass.

"To Drunksie, atta girl," Phoebe counters as we clink glasses.

I arrive at work the next morning, Halloween, ready to send out media kits for our annual buyers' guide. The normal protocol maintains temps be made available in order that the media kits for the guides be put together and mailed appropriately as it's quite the time-consuming task. Alas, no temps can be found this morning. Not even a single temp appears.

Phoebe, from her cubicle a few over from mine, questions, "Where are the temps?"

Lynette replies over the cubicle walls, "Ryan's not hiring the temps for us. He was supposed to, he was going to, at least that's what he said all of last week."

Phoebe implores, "But we can't do this ourselves, there is too much to be done. The buyers' guide kits have to be made and sent. Why isn't he getting the temps?"

Commence the yelling from Lynette. Lynette screams, "If YOU (*points directly at Phoebe*) would've given HIM (*points directly at Ryan's office*) a blowjob last night we would have had our temps. That's where our temps are!"

If it were later in the day, and we were in the suburbs, I would be able to hear crickets in the office, such is the silence after this explosion.

Ryan occasionally lets his gaze linger on Phoebe a few seconds too long, but Phoebe, however, is betrothed. In addition, she's about two decades younger than Ryan. It's probable herein lies the allure Phoebe has to Ryan. Regardless, Ryan doesn't hire the temps and so Phoebe, Lynette, and I prepare to work feverishly on the media kits for the annual buyers' guide.

"If I blew him we would've had our temps, I can't believe she thinks that," Phoebe claims just when Lynette steps away.

"Phoebe," I begin, "you know, for a fact, that Ryan wants you in the worst way. We totally would've had our temps. It's all right though. You don't have to sell yourself, even if it is for a temp or two. You could have though. Theoretically."

Phoebe glares at me in response.

"Just kidding," I tell her, and then follow it up with a shallowly whispered, "No, I'm not."

Phoebe, in preparation for a morning filled with the monotonous preparation of media kits, sits at her cubicle and begins to consume baby carrots. Phoebe maintains a vegan lifestyle and has an orange color to her skin. I swear her skin is orange because of the insane amount of carrots she eats every day. At least, in terms of duration of chomping, it sounds like a full bag a day. She doesn't sit for a couple of minutes, eat her carrots, and move on. That would be too easy. Instead, she takes her time while she eats each one. She can get about four or five bites out of each baby carrot, while I could probably eat each of the carrots in one or two bites. After all, they're baby carrots, not the full-grown, bugs-bunny type of carrots.

The sound gets under my skin like nothing else. The snapping of each baby carrot makes my vertebrae tense up one by one, starting at the base of my spine and steadily moving upward, tensing, until my posture radically changes and my shoulders arch back. To hear Phoebe sitting behind me, eating, one by one, each of those tiny baby carrots, day after day, completely unnerves me. I walk around the office to get away from the sound. Sometimes I go to get water. Other times I take a stroll to the bathroom. I will do anything to avoid the incessant crunching and snapping of those baby carrots.

I stroll on over to the fridge to put in a bottle of pomegranate juice for later when, what do my eyes alight on, but none other than a bag of those fucking baby carrots. Carrots, I think, these must be more of Phoebe's carrots. The bane of my existence. I love Phoebe, but God how I hate these carrots. Anyway, I finish in the kitchen and walk to the bathroom to wash my hands and check the mirror. I fix my hair, adjust my tie, and give myself one last look in the mirror. I place both of my hands on the countertop, fingers splayed, and stare at myself in the mirror. I say, "I think I can do it. I can do it. Do it. Do it fast, and get it done." Okay self, here goes nothing. Out through the bathroom door, a sharp right, another sharp right, I open the fridge, grab the bag of carrots, whirl around, and in one quick dunk I slam the offending bag of carrots through the swinging lid of the receptacle. The flip, flip, flipping of the lid heralds an unparalleled happiness. There will be no more carrot chomping today. I love Phoebe, but I've had enough of those fucking carrots.

Perhaps Phoebe's oral fixation for carrots is what enticed Ryan at the office party.

Charlie Casso

Halloween, my favorite day of the year, is finally here. Better than Christmas, better than my birthday, better than every and any other day: Halloween. No matter what I'm doing in life, or what my age, for this one day of the year I can be anyone or anything I want to be and I can be a complete kid about it. Want to be a doctor? No problem. Want to be a monster? No problem. How about a spaceman, Frankenstein's creation, or a member of the opposite sex? My options are unlimited. My inner child is allowed this one day a year to come out and play without recourse.

Now, with a recent break-up right before Halloween and Halloween being my favorite holiday, I hope this night becomes a night to remember. I hop on the local train to Phoebe's apartment after work to get ready for New York's Greenwich Village Halloween Parade. My costume consists of a full rabbit outfit my mom has spent months creating. The intricacies of the head to toe white fur body, white-with-pink-inside rabbit ears, white-with-pink-inside hand-mitts, fluffy cottontail, and over-sized carrot combine to make one spectacle of an outfit. The irony of my costume dawns on me, me as a rabbit with my recent carrot issues at work. I love it all the more.

At Phoebe's sixth floor walk-up apartment, with grand views of a brick wall (at least there are windows,) Phoebe tears open two packets of Hurricane mix and empties the contents into a yellow, plastic pitcher, the likes of which remind me of my childhood in the '80s. I pull on the pieces of the rabbit costume until I'm a fully outfitted, head-to-toe, rabbit.

Phoebe puts the final touches on the Hurricanes as she stirs the red mixture into a whirlpool inside the yellow pitcher. Phoebe pours the drinks into two large pink tumblers, to which I can't help but ask, "Jeez, Phoebe, '80s much?"

She replies, "You know you love it. And they were ninety-nice cents each, so yeah."

On the outskirts of her kitchenette, since the size of it doesn't allow for two people, she hands me my tumbler and raises a toast. "To Halloween, Hurricanes, and…and… Hoo-wah."

"Pacino, huh?" I ask, "Well, cheers on hoo-wah. One, two, three…"

Together we give a raspy growl of "hoo-wah," bump our tumblers together, and drink. We recline on Phoebe's twin-size bed, which doubles as the couch, while we wait for John and throw a few drinks back. More accurately, Phoebe throws one or two back, while I have, well, more than two.

By the time John arrives at her apartment to drive us downtown to the parade, I'm already three sheets to the wind. "How much did you drink?" he asks me.

"I only had this one tumbler since I got here," I truthfully answer.

"Josh, that's true," Phoebe starts, as she give me a telling look, "but how many refills did you have?"

"Happy Halloween!" I exclaim, while at just about the same time John starts to utter, "Oh, Lord."

The car ride zooms right by. I wave at people in another car who, by the amused looks on their faces, can't believe a giant rabbit hops around the back seat. After I wave to them, I lay myself down. The next thing I know, I pee on a tree in public. Then I'm on the ground. I lie on the ground, face down, in the middle of the sidewalk on Christopher Street. I roll over to find a cop standing over me. Not a Halloween-outfitted cop. A real cop.

"Hello, offi-hiccup-offisssir," I slur.

The cop replies, "Is someone having too happy a Halloween?"

"Yeah, well," Phoebe explains, "he's had a stressful couple of weeks officer, he's a good guy."

"I am. Good Guy. Yep. Tell that to Steven, not sure to stay or go. I'll be fine. And Ry-hiccup-an."

The cop asks, "Who's Steven? Are you Steven?"

"No, I'm John."

"Steven's his ex," Phoebe explains.

"Then who's Ryan?"

Phoebe clarifies, "Ryan's his boss' boss."

"Offisssssser," I ask, "do you know Ry-hiccup-an and Steven?"

"No, I don't believe I do."

"Aww nuts. If you find 'em, lock 'em up. They bad peoples. Baaaad peeeeples."

John tries to explain, "He works downtown, officer. He just had a break up, and work has been stressful. He just drank too much tonight. We're going to take him home right now. We got this, I promise."

"Ahh, that explains it. Don't worry, the bad peoples won't hurt you anymore. You just take care of yourself. That sound good?"

"Yes. Hap… errr. Hap.. pee Halloweeen mista officer."

"Well, he's definitely a happy drunk, that's for sure. All right, take him home. Be safe."

"Definitely," John promises.

Finally, I lie down in the back of John's car. He calls my mom, tells her he will bring me home, and brings me home. I single-handedly ruin Halloween. I sit on my mom's front porch as she tries to get me to come inside. I plead, "Please leave me alone." I have blown it completely. A ruined Halloween, the recent end of a relationship, and 364 days left until the next time I will get a chance at my favorite holiday. And of course, asking my mom to leave me alone while I'm intoxicated and dressed like a rabbit doesn't mark a high point either.

Halloween, one month and twenty days after 9/11, appears to be rock-bottom. So even though the night ends with a whimper, I still have a great souvenir from Louisiana to think about: Angelo.

Chapter Fifteen: Mister Officer Was Right, Bad Peoples No More

From: Angelo
To: Josh
Sent: 11/2/01
Subject: GOOBER!!!!!

I can't believe you emailed me from your old email address to give me your new one and forgot to include it! It makes me glad to know that someone else can be as blonde as me at times. Thankfully you remembered to email me from the address you use. I'm usually running around the office, so I'm better at emailing than at phone conversations, at least while at work. Well, I got to work with every intention of running and loading up on caffeine, but of course the phone starts ringing and everyone has a problem. When will they realize that I really don't care about their issues? LOL. So, I can imagine what kind of day you are having there in the big city. I hope you slept well. I did, until the power went out in the middle of the night and the alarm system went crazy because of it. Yes, the night from HELL! That's why I wanted to load up on caffeine this morning. But I made it through. "I'M A SURVIVOR!"

You know something, speaking of sleep, one of the things I miss most about being with someone is falling asleep holding him, or falling asleep being held, and waking up and watching him sleep. Smooch!!!!!

P.S. I'm so happy I took my niece to the aquarium yesterday. She brightened my day and all I had to do was feed her McDonald's and buy her a stuffed animal whenever she squealed, "Unkie Angelo, this is so cute!"

Angelo Welles
Technology Coordinator

* * *

From: Josh
To: Angelo
Sent: 11/2/01
Subject: Milkud!!!!!

Hey MilkDud LOL,

Sorry about the email address thing. Yeah, I told you
that I, too, have my blonde moments. I was going to title
the email that contained the email address "Whoops" but
then I said, nah, I'll just leave the title blank, thinking that
it wouldn't look like I had a ditzy moment. Then I
received your response. I've never been called a Goober
before, so when I saw that I just started laughing. And
I've decided to call you MilkDud; it has a cute ring to it.
But don't worry, I don't think MilkDud would go over too
well as a term of affection. We'll see. Very cute regarding
your niece, by the way, very cute. She calls you Unkie
Angelo, awww. What a good Uncle you must be. If I had
taken my niece to go to the aquarium in the French
Quarter I would not have fed her McDonald's. I would
have been like, "Here are your beignets, and here is your
cafe au lait." Although, there is a good chance that my
niece would just play with her beignets while I ate mine.
Then we would wind up three minutes later in a
McDonald's ordering a happy meal for her, hoping she
wouldn't see that I snuck the toy out of the box to call it
my own. Kidding. I would never take a toy away from

my niece. Well, unless it was a Britney Spears toy. (We all have our limits, don't we?)

LOL and MWAH. U R 2 Cute.
Josh

* * *

From: Angelo
To: Josh
Sent: 11/2/01
Subject: Re: Milkdud!!!!!

MILKDUD?????? I am dying over here!!! I'm on a total caffeine buzz right now. I am laughing my ass off at the MILKDUD thing too. No one has ever responded that way to me calling them Goober. I LOVE IT! But I do agree, it is not a good term of affection. That would be one of those nicknames that would make me want to gag if I heard someone else using it. I hate cheesy, lovey-dovey couples. Don't get me wrong, I will hold hands and kiss you in public to a limit. But I really don't over do the PDA (public display of affection). To me, when a couple is doing all that, it's like they are trying too hard to prove a point. Know what I mean? And, why would I want to mack down on you in public anyways? I'd rather do it somewhere secluded, just the two of us, so it can be done right and lead to whatever. Ok, I just so went off on a tangent. Excuse the blonde streaks please. LOL MilkDud. I'm dying over here, you Goober! Smooch!!!!
P.S.
I'm sexy, I'm cute ... and popular to boot!

Angelo Welles
Technology Coordinator

* * *

From: Angelo
To: Josh
Sent: 11/2/01
Subject: Re: Milkdud!!!!!

    Oh and just so you know, you have to quit making me smile. It's totally ruining my bitch facade here at work.

    Oh My God, I am so having an allergic reaction to something. My arm is itching and I am getting hives. I can't have an allergic reaction right now, I have too much to do between work and my home improvement projects at night!

    So what is your middle name Josh Conti? I don't think I asked you that yet.

Smooch!!!
Angelo Welles
Technology Coordinator

* * *

From: Josh
To: Angelo
Sent: 11/2/01
Subject: Good Afternoon

Hey,

Charles. So, the JC works well with both the middle and the last name.

Hmm, as for the allergic reaction, it must have been something you ate for lunch. Was it pizza? Sometimes the sauce, depending on the place and the person, gives people hives. Or you could be allergic to home improvement. The latter makes more sense, doesn't it?

Feel better Angelo,
MWAH
JC

* * *

From: Angelo
To: Josh
Sent: 11/2/01
Subject: Re: Good Afternoon

Most likely it's the dust. I like your response though, it's what I'd expect a New Yorker's response to be, asking me if I had pizza. I wish I did have a slice of New York pizza, or a pizza-burger! I have been allergic to dust for as long as I can remember. But I'll be ok. And before you ask, my house is usually very clean. Should we live together one day, you'll be very impressed. I make a mean breakfast, lunch, and dinner. All of your N'awlins favorites. You really have to try my biscuits with gravy, and that's not a euphemism for anything sexual, lol. To die for, I swear!

JC (Jesus Christ). Ok, I had a blonde moment. Charles has a nice ring to it, but calling you "the other

JC" makes me laugh too. Anyways, I'll give you a call tonight. I have to run around for a little bit here and take care of some computer issues. At least I have tonight to look forward to.

Be careful my New York City boy, and I'll talk to you later.
Smooch!!!
Angelo

* * *

From: Angelo
To: Josh
Sent: 11/5/01
Subject: Smooch

I know we talked about meeting up in Houston in a few weeks when you have your client meetings, but I was going to say you might want to check out coming here for Mardi Gras since you've never seen it. We'll get you some beads!

Let me know around what time you normally take lunch. If we overlap our lunch times, we can get some phone time in during the day.

Smooch!!!
Angelo

* * *

From: Josh
To: Angelo
Sent: 11/5/01
To: Angelo Welles
Subject: smooch / pet names

Hey MilkDud (I'm sorry, but it is kind of cute :O)

The day is just flying by. I had a bunch of misdirected calls too, which is unusual. Lunch hour for me varies. I usually go between 12:30 and 2:30 for an hour, depending on when I feel hungry or when I feel that I need some sunshine.

Speaking of which, I'm going to go to the travel agent at lunch just to see if she can get any good deals on a Mardi Gras- time trip for me to come to see you. It's still early enough where something decently priced might be possible. (At least I hope.) I was going to say, if you wanted to go to Las Vegas, I already have a hotel room booked for my Britney trip, and it's only for a weekend. I arrive in Las Vegas a little before midnight on Thursday, Nov. 15, and leave on a flight out on Sunday, Nov 18th, at 11:59 p.m. I figure I would put the option out there if it is somewhere you have an interest in going, although I don't know what the availability of Britney tickets is. There's a show on Saturday night and one on Sunday afternoon. Yes, I'm going to both.

I also know that you'd go to Houston when I have to go there on a business trip, which would be totally great and all. Well, what I'm trying to say is if it is something you want to do you are more than welcome.

Otherwise, I will just see you in Houston :0) I hope this email makes sense to you. It should.

I'm going to see Monsters Inc. right after work with Phoebe today, after which I'll jet home to pack for my business trip tomorrow. HeeYay. Sarcasm is intended though on the packing part.

Hope you're having a good day, my little MilkDud. God, how I would have loved to have seen your face when you read "MilkDud" for the first time. :0)

Josh

* * *

From: Angelo
To: Josh
Sent: 11/5/01
Subject: (No pet name as of yet)

I checked airline tickets to Las Vegas. On such short notice, I'd be looking at 300 bucks for a ticket. That, along with the fact I don't think I am going to my parents' house for Thanksgiving leads me to the conclusion I will be going to see them that weekend. I wish I could go meet you there though. But, I guess I will see you in Houston the following weekend or close to there.

Oh, I am buying *Legally Blonde* on the way home tonight. I can't wait to see it again.
Actually, what I can't wait for is to sit with you and watch a movie together. :)
"Who am I, just guess ... guys wanna touch my chest"

Smooch!!!
Angelo

* * *

From: Angelo
To: Josh
Sent: 11/5/01
Subject: CD

Hey, you. I forgot I have a question I needed to ask. You wouldn't, by any chance, want the new Britney Spears CD before it's released would you? Or has it already been released up there? I like a little Britney every now and then, and I know you definitely love you some Britney.

Smooch!!!
Angelo Welles

* * *

From: Josh
To: Angelo
Sent: 11/5/01
Subject: CD / names

Milkdud,

The Britney CD comes out tomorrow, but I purchased it on Saturday. One of the independent music stores by my house always gets their CDs a couple of days early. (Thank you though.)
Oh, and by the way, I already thought of this: you can't call me "Goober" for the same reasons that we already spoke about, namely, the *Legally Blonde* thing

wherein the guy called Reese Witherspoon "Pooh Bear" then called his new girlfriend "Pooh Bear" as well. You yourself said that you can't go around calling different people the same thing. Well, as per your email to me, you stated that when you called other people "Goober" in the past, no one responded like I did. (You see where I am going with this-- you've already applied it to others.) So there :0) And, FYI, "Chunky" is not appropriate, and should we one day be in bed together, exclaiming "Oh Henry" would not be acceptable either.

Went to the travel agency... yikes. Airfare on JetBlue is $330, which is not too bad, but my last trip was $189. As for hotels, they have the Fairfield, which isn't even in the French Quarter, at $208 per night. Since it's both Mardi Gras and Superbowl time they could only offer the hotel rates, no discount. So, I guess I'll see what happens. The hotel I stayed in at last check had two rooms available at $210 per night, and that's in the quarter, so I'd much rather stay there. I'll wait to see if you find out anything. Maybe tonight I'll go online to see if I can find a cheaper airfare myself.

Till later, MWAH.
Josh

* * *

From: Angelo
To: Josh
Sent: 11/5/01
Subject: Re: CD / names

Well, technically, it could apply. See the term "Goober" wasn't used in a term of endearment kind of way. I usually call everyone Goober at some point. So, this actually makes you the first person I have used it on in an affectionate sort of way. But, if you like, I can always go with Twix, Snickers, Raisinette, Butter Finger, Skittle, Mounds, Almond Joy, Peanut Butter Cup, Whatchamacallit, etc. Just let me know which appeals to you. :) Although, no matter what you choose, the decision is up to me. It is my prerogative to choose the pet name I have for you. And be careful what you choose to call me because payback is a bitch. :) I guess it all depends on what feels right when I call you something. We'll see.

Hmmm, you don't seem like a Pooh Bear either. I'll need some time to process this one.
Oh, and don't worry about me screaming out "Oh Henry" when we are in bed...
I usually scream out my own name because I am just that damn good! Ok, I couldn't resist. I crack myself up sometimes. Oh, and as for the cd, I guess I am totally downloading all these songs for nothing since you already have the cd. Oh well, my niece will think I am the biggest hero ever when I give it to her.

Smooch! ! !
Angelo

From: Josh
To: Angelo
Sent: 11/5/01
Subject: What's in a name?

M.D., (and that does not stand for Doctor,)

Well, I figured I'd put the Las Vegas option out there just in case, you never know.

Nice of you to check though :0) We'll work out a plan for Houston, Mardi Gras, who knows what else. Hey, maybe dating someone who doesn't live in the same state may wind up opening up entirely new experiences, for both of us. The world's our oyster to crack open.

As for the Britney CD, I certainly hope you're making a copy of it for yourself. It's really good. Actually, instead of making a copy, buy the real CD, artwork and all. Not only is it an amazing album, but buying it will do wonders for your karma.

Oh, and as for my pet name, of course it is up to you to call me what you like. Although, out of the candy bar names you mentioned, Peanut Butter Cup is the name of my aunt's dead dog, so that's not good, Raisinette is too effeminate, and Mounds just doesn't sound right. And I'm not Chinese, so please don't call me Almond Joy. LOL.

But you've got all of the time in the world to come up with a name. It's like, one day you'll go to call me or email me and the name will just pop out of your mouth. Similar to how everything else happens in life, this too will just happen. And that's when you'll know that it's right.

MWAH –JC

www.ingramcontent.com/pod-product-compliance
Lightning Source LLC
Chambersburg PA
CBHW05203226O626
47163CB00006B/197